WHEN
BIRDS
TAKE
FLIGHT

Finlandia Foundation National
Grant Recipient
2020

SUSANNA KRIZO

When Birds Take Flight
Copyright © 2021 Susanna Krizo

ISBN: 9781976306822

"Minä olen kerran ja toisen ajatellut miksi et pane kampsut pussihin ja lähde tänne – en minä usko että sun sitä tarvitsee koskaan katua. Vuosi pari aukaisis sinun silmäs täällä enempi kuin 20t sielä."

Kirje Yhdysvalloista
Vaasaan vuonna 1909

"I have wondered more than once why you don't pack your things and come over here – I don't think you will ever have to regret it. A year or two here will open your eyes more than twenty years over there."

Letter from Finnish Immigrant to
Vaasa, Finland 1909

Glossary of Finnish & Spanish
Words and phrases found in this novel
Is located at the end of the book

Decision Time
(April 19, 2018)

We all think life is going to be simple, that things are always going to turn out the way we think they will; and yet, we all know life doesn't work that way. John Lennon was right, life happens while we make other plans.

I had a plan. Or, I should say, I had a dream. My dream was beautiful, so beautiful I didn't ever want to wake up.

And I didn't.

Life ripped my dream apart and sent me to the world of nightmares where nothing is ever beautiful. Life didn't ask me if I wanted to end up there and of course it didn't. Life doesn't ask. It gives and takes without considering what we think about it.

And yet, I know life can be beautiful too, just like our dreams; it does give us what we want and need. The only trouble is that life is unpredictable in every way. And because it's unpredictable, finding answers when we need them is like staring at an ever-expanding lake that hides more than it reveals. Sometimes we get the answers right by guessing, but mostly we find ourselves staring at the vast expanse trying to find if there are right answers to begin with.

I thought I had found one of the answers. I thought coming here was the beginning of a new story, a love story. And perhaps it was a love story; it just didn't come with a happy ending. Or maybe I was just too blind to see what was right in front of me because love blinds us. Marriage opens our eyes because marriage isn't a love story; it's a life story. It's a story of a life lived together, for better or for worse, and sometimes the better just isn't there no matter how hard we try to find it.

We all have expectations when we marry. My marriage to Greg was like an expectation that never materialized. I waited and waited, and every time I thought I was getting *really* close to making it work, the rug was pulled from underneath my feet and I was back looking at the promised end-result from a distance wondering, "Why the hell did I marry this person?"

I don't have to ask that question anymore.

Our marriage ended today.

I know I'm supposed to feel sad, but mostly I just feel relieved and a little bit like a loser, although I guess I shouldn't feel that way. We all think we're supposed to be experts when it comes to love, but none of us are. We're not even experts when it comes to our own lives. We all fail lots of times and we're all left feeling like losers. Finns tried to fix this feeling with the slogan, *"Elämästä ei anneta arvosanaa; your life isn't graded."* It told every Finn they couldn't fail in life because life has no exams that can be graded.

I'm not so sure it's true.

Life asks us questions and expects us to answer. The question life asked me two and half years ago was whether love was worth leaving everything I knew behind.

I thought I knew the answer.

I had no idea.

I remember reading Juho August Hollo when I was barely eighteen. He said, *"Oma tyhmyyteni on minulle tärkeämpi kuin vieras viisaus; my own stupidity is more important to me than a stranger's wisdom."* I thought it sounded so wise then, but perhaps it wasn't. I could have used a stranger's wisdom to counter my own stupidity.

Moving to Chicago was the bravest thing I've ever done. It was also the most stupid thing I have ever done. I wanted to prove to myself that I could be brave.

That was the stupid part.

I've never been brave. I wasn't brave in Finland where everything was familiar and simple. Why did I think I was going to be able to be brave on this side of the ocean, where everything is different and complicated, where everything makes me feel like I don't belong because I wasn't born here? Being an immigrant is like walking uphill against the wind on a good day; on a bad day it makes you feel as if you're homeless, at the mercy of the elements. But at the same time I'm not so sure I want to return to the listless familiarity that was my life in Finland. My life at home was safe—too safe; nothing ever happened. It's as if I can only have one or the other.

I know I have to make a decision now that I'm no longer married. I have to decide whether I want to stay here or go back home to Finland. I know Miguel wants me to stay and I love him more than anything in this world, but I don't know if I want to be an immigrant all my life. I don't know if I want to spend the rest of my life on the outside looking in, never feeling at home. My future depends on a decision I don't know how to make.

That's not true.

It's a decision I don't want to make.

Maybe the best thing—the only thing—I can do right now is to see if the answer is somewhere in the past. Maybe a stranger had some wise words for me and I didn't hear them the first time around. I have to be wiser this time. I can't let my heart make the decision for me.

Not this time.

1

I press my card against the card reader. A big white "X" with the text "Insufficient Funds" stares back at me.

"*Voi vittu!*"

The words slip out before I have a chance to stop them. The driver gives me a curious glance. He doesn't know what the words mean. He wouldn't have cared even if he did. He's only curious because he didn't recognize the language.

I pull my phone from my pocket. I click on the Ventra app and wait and wait and—nothing. I don't have any cash on me and the Ventra app seems to hate my phone or maybe it's my phone that hates the app. It doesn't matter which way it is, I can't pay. The driver's frown tells me he has a schedule to keep, so could I please just pay or get off.

I sit back down on the short narrow bench under the see-through shelter. The cold wind nips my cheeks, although it's only October. Heavy rains ended summer abruptly two weeks ago and made the city look like a woman in mourning. I'm mourning too, but not for someone who's dead. He's still here, somewhere in this city. I just don't know where he is.

I stare at the wet street that has become a river of shimmering lights. I used to love playing on the street outside of our home as a kid after it had rained. The water remained clear under my feet and formed into pearls as my feet flung it up into the air.

This street is different. It's not meant for playing. It's cold and long, and it stretches from one end of the city to the other. It takes me to work and home again.

Home.

Where is my home? It's not here, but it's not on the other side of the ocean either. I feel just as homeless as the old woman I see pushing a stroller filled with overflowing plastic bags. I know I'm not, but everything in me tells me I am.

My vision becomes blurry suddenly. I wipe my eyes and tell myself to stop thinking about it; it will only lead to longing. I glance at the lit windows across the street. The light reminds me I will be longing for my apartment too unless I can get to it somehow. Twenty miles is about thirty kilometers, I count. It's not impossible. I've done it before. But stepping on a soft forest floor isn't the same as walking on hard asphalt and I don't like the idea of walking in the dark by myself.

Not in this city.

I pull my phone from my pocket and click on the Ventra app again. The circle goes around and around and—yes! The site pops up on the screen. I add ten dollars to my account and hit submit. The pop-up tells me I have now 11 dollars and 25 cents on my account. I smile at my phone and slide it back into my pocket.

The smile lingers on my lips. It dies a second later when I realize I haven't smiled since Greg left. I waited for him for days. In the end I realized he wasn't coming back.

That was a month ago.

I hear a sudden loud slam and turn to look. I watch as a man charges like an angry bull toward the car in front of him.

"When the *fuck* are you going to move?"

"Shut up!" yells the woman through the open car window. She gives the man an angry stare and gets out of her car. She waves her arms as if asking the man to look around. "Can't you see the cars aren't moving? I'll move when I can!"

The man huffs, turns around, and charges back to his car. He drives around the woman's car and turns to Chicago Avenue with a screech. I watch as he gets stuck behind another car. He's not going anywhere. No one gets anywhere in this city—other than tourists. They have a merry time visiting. I know they do, because I was once one of them.

I turn my head just in time to see two young women approach the crosswalk. They giggle.

"I love Chicago!" shouts one of them, raising her hands toward the sky.

I watch as they cross the street. I want to run after them and ask if they would still love the city if the man had pulled a gun on the woman in the car.

It happens where I live.

The bus arrives.

I find an empty seat and sit down. I glance at the man next to me; he smells like booze.

"I don't get it! How did *that* happen?" mumbles the man angrily. "What! I don't get it!"

I wonder who he is talking to until I realize there's no one at the other end of the line; he's talking to himself.

"I'm claustrophobic," says the man, giving me a wide drunken smile. "I'm all right. I just have to conquer my fears. I know how to conquer my fears, I know how to do it," mumbles the man, nodding slowly.

He stretches his back and begins to sing loudly.

"Hey man, tone it down!" shouts the driver.

The man stops singing.

"Did you hear that? We can't sing here," says the man to his phone.

"La Salle!" calls the driver.

"*La Salle!* Let me get out at LaSalle!" shouts the man, jumping up to his feet. He pushes people to the side as he makes his way to the front.

"You all make me feel—I'm claustrophobic! I need to get out! Let me out of here!"

I watch as the man pushes the people standing by the door aside and steps on the pavement with unsteady legs. I can still hear his drunken mumbling as he walks away from the bus. A feeling of pity fills me. Some people have only themselves to talk to in this city.

The chatter around me intensifies. I glance at the people around me. The atmosphere is jovial, although more than one person shows signs of weariness. The bus driver rests his hand on the horn more than once. Maybe it's the traffic that is annoying him or maybe his day is almost over and he wants to be home already.

I can't wait to be home too, put my feet up and eat pizza. That frozen pizza has become the highlight of my day makes me gloomy for a moment, but at least I have the pizza. It's more than many of my neighbors have. I know I should be grateful, but something in me keeps telling me it's insane I have to be grateful to have enough to eat.

The land of the free and the home of the brave.

The only thing people are free to be here is brave; brave before hunger and insurmountable odds.

The bus stops at a red light. I turn to look out the window and see an old couple get out of a taxi. I wonder again how it's possible for some people to stay together their whole lives while others don't make it past their first year of marriage. I don't have an answer, I don't think anyone does. Love is what we all want and need, but sometimes we just can't make it work no matter how hard we try. We all hope love will last and that life will caress us endlessly with soft petals. In reality, love ends and life pokes us mercilessly until we either give up or harden ourselves. To deal with the pain some people turn either to religion or addiction, and although one side prays and the other drinks or inhales, the net result is the same—they escape reality.

I can understand why people look for a way to end the pain, but I'm convinced religion isn't the best solution. My experience is limited to a specific church in a specific neighborhood, but I always thought it was filled with a bunch of people with a massive need to control everyone around them. When people didn't fall in line, they were threatened with punishment. That's church for you. It's like being married to a narcissist. I have first-hand proof of it, because I'm married to one.

Or was.

Still am.

I don't know what I am anymore.

The bus glides effortlessly down Chicago Avenue as soon as we leave downtown. Twenty minutes later the cheery mechanical voice announces we are approaching Springfield Avenue.

I pull the cord and get off the bus. I begin to walk down the dark street. Only the yellow glare from the streetlights provides light and it isn't much. I see a rat running across the street. I wait for it to disappear behind a building. I wonder again whose brainless idea it was to get rid of all the feral cats. Now the whole city is infested with rats; plump, intrepid rats entirely unafraid of humans. And why should they be afraid? We don't have sharp teeth we can sink into their necks; instead we feed them with our trash. They must think we're their best friends.

I open the gate and unlock the door to my apartment. I see my cat appear from the darkness. It meows and pushes its head against my leg.

"*Hei, oliko sulla ikävä*? Did you miss me?" I say and pet its head. My cat purrs and continues to push its head against my leg.

I throw my bag on the couch and walk to the kitchen. I open a can of cat food, turn on the oven and plop the frozen pizza into the cold oven. I pour myself a glass of wine and watch as my cat eats its food eagerly.

It's just me and my cat now. I don't know anyone in this city anymore other than my co-workers and we're not friends. The women hate me for some reason and the men just want to hook up. Perhaps the reason the women hate me is because the men want me and not them. I want to tell them they can have the men—all of them. I'm not interested in American men anymore. I'm not interested in men, period.

I sip my wine and think about my new reality. Two years ago I would have been okay with being this alone; just me and my thoughts. Now all I want is to escape my thoughts and be with other people.

I finish the first glass quickly and pour myself another. I down the second glass just as quickly. I want my thoughts to disappear into the haze of intoxication although I know there is no point to it, because on the other side waits handsome self-absorbed Greg and all the reasons I'm alone in this city.

There is no escape.

2

I can feel something touching my face.

I open my eyes.

My cat is pawing my cheek. It puts its paw back down, tilts its head and looks at me with its solemn eyes; they ask when I'm going to get up.

I sit up slowly. My head pounds and my tongue feels like a big fat blob in my mouth. Yesterday's mascara has formed into tear-soaked clumps on my lashes. I must have cried myself to sleep again.

My cat jumps on the floor and begins to walk toward the kitchen. It turns its head and looks at me to see if I'm following.

"I know, I know, you're hungry," I say and get up.

I walk slowly to the kitchen. I fill the cat's bowl with dry cat food and make coffee for myself. I know it's not healthy, this daily back-and-forth between the glass and the mug, but I don't know what else to do. I can't stay awake without coffee and I can't go to sleep without wine. I no longer wonder why people become addicted. It's not just about escaping pain. If we can't connect with some*one*, we connect with some*thing*. We don't necessarily want the substance; we want the feeling of satisfaction that comes from having a steady supply of either ecstasy or oblivion in the absence of human love.

My cat jumps on the counter and pushes its head against

my arm. I know it's only looking for attention, but cats don't belong on kitchen counters; that's at least what my grandmother always said. I pick it up and rub my nose against its nose.

"Is this what you wanted?"

My cat gives me an annoyed look as if to say "no." I scratch the space behind its left ear.

"*Parempi?* Yeah, that's better."

I watch as my cat closes its eyes and begins to purr softly. Cats are like narcissists. They make everyone else feel guilty while they are the ones who act like assholes. Why anyone puts up with it is just another unsolved mystery. Perhaps we accept their behavior because they give us love. But it's not love, not really. Love should be there all the time, not just sometimes.

Naming the cat was the first argument Greg and I ever had. Greg wanted to call the cat Whiskey, but I didn't think it was such a good idea. I imagined myself saying, "Have you seen Whiskey?" to the neighbors who can be found drinking on the porch most days. Greg told me I was being paranoid and refused to call the cat anything else, so I just called it "cat." I still do. It doesn't seem to mind.

I put my cat down on the floor. I notice the cereal box on top of the fridge; it's Greg's favorite brand. I left it there, just in case he decided to come back.

He didn't.

Sometimes I think he'll come back, but I know it's not true. He's left me and our marriage.

I stare out the window for a moment.

If only I had stayed home that night two years ago instead of going to Sara's party I would never have met Greg and I would never have come here; I would have stayed in Finland.

It's funny how one decision can change everything.

Absolutely everything.

. . . . . . ● . . . . .

I heard my phone ring as I stepped out of the shower. I rushed to the living room wrapped in a towel and grabbed my phone. It was Sara. She wanted to know when I was coming; the party had already started. I bit my lip and mumbled something about the weather.

"Sä oot kuin meiän mummo! Nyt pistät hameen päälle ja tuut tänne."

I wanted to tell her she was right. I felt old; old at the age of twenty-two, but I knew she didn't want to hear it.

I closed my eyes briefly.

"Ok, mä tuun."

I hung up and went to the bedroom. I knew there was no arguing with Sara when she was in this mood. I pulled a black skirt and a white sweater from the closet and threw them on the bed. Just because I had to go to the party didn't mean I had to make an effort to look nice.

The rain whipped my face as I strolled down the damp street. I pulled my umbrella closer to prevent it from taking off. These parties were always the same. People drank too much, swore they would never drink again, only to repeat the same the next weekend. I couldn't see the point with it anymore. I had tried to explain to Sara why I hated these parties, but she just looked at me with her soft blue eyes and told me to stop being childish. I knew she was determined to get me back to the world of the living no matter what I thought about. It didn't matter how many times I told her I wanted to be left alone, she just shook her head and told me I should start dating again as soon as possible according to her therapy books; it wasn't healthy to spend as much time alone as I did after a breakup. I already knew it wasn't going to happen. All of the men I knew thought they were perfectly irresistible once they had downed enough vodka, obviously convinced their smarmy compliments and groping would turn any woman on. I found them all revolting.

I opened the door to the stairwell. I climbed the stairs and rang the doorbell. Sara screamed as she opened the door and saw me. She gave me a hug and told me she was happy I had finally decided to show up. I gave her a brief smile and stepped into the small hallway. I watched as Sara danced toward the living room with her drink high above her head. She had already had enough to drink although it wasn't even nine.

I sighed.

It was going to be a long night.

I took off my coat and shoes. The mountain of coats on the coatrack smelled like a wet ashtray. I didn't want my coat to catch the smell, so I folded it and put it under the table hoping it would be safe there from wet shoes and vomit.

I was about to walk into the living room when I heard loud laughter rippling from the end of the room.

I stopped.

An American.

I wondered who could possibly have invited him. A second later I realized it had to be Sara's husband, Samuli. He was the only one who had friends all over the world due to his work. I had no desire to spend the evening listening to an arrogant American; it was bad enough I had to be at the party in the first place. I took a few steps back, turned around, and walked into the kitchen.

I sat down by the table and looked at the assortment of bottles. Most of them were already half-empty. I poured myself a drink and wondered how long I would have to stay. I figured an hour should be enough to make Sara happy. She would complain about me leaving early, but I could always claim I had a headache. It wouldn't be a complete lie, not with the music blasting from the living room at maximum volume.

I finished my drink and poured myself another. I listened as the music changed abruptly from rock to tango; someone was feeling sentimental. My dad used to always marvel at Finns and their love for tango. He said it was odd that people who were as cold as the arctic weather tangoed all summer long under the starless sky like the Argentinians. As I got older I concluded it was the silence of the passion that appealed to the people. They didn't have to talk. All they had to do was move to the music. It was kind of like having sex with clothes on.

A young woman with braided hair and minimal makeup came into the kitchen. She didn't look at me as she poured herself a drink. I didn't care. I knew she was one of Sara's university friends. I didn't know any of them. They all lived in a different world.

A moment later a spindly young man stumbled into the kitchen. He flopped down on the chair next to me and examined my face through narrowed eyes. His eyes widened as if he had just realized something upsetting.

"*Katriina, perkele! Sunhan piti auttaa mua ennen tenttiä! Minne helvettiin sä katosit?*"

I told the drunken young man my name wasn't Katriina and that I hadn't been accepted into the university when I had applied three years ago. His eyes turned into slivers and he wagged his finger at me as if telling me he knew I was lying, that I was only saying it because I hadn't helped him although I had promised to do so.

I let out a deep sigh and stared at the kitchen cabinets. Drunken people were depressing, depressed drunken people even more so. As if the young man had read my thoughts, he began a grainy monologue about the brilliance of his thesis and how his professor hadn't understood him. The monologue morphed into a tear-filled lament as the young man explained between the sobs how he had failed, how his life was over. Perhaps I should have felt sorry for him, but I couldn't.

I wished I had been given a chance to fail too.

The young man fell asleep. I watched as his head sank and landed precariously close to the edge of the table. I left him to his self-inflicted grief and went to the living room. I swept the room quickly with my eyes. When I couldn't spot anyone who looked like an American I sat down on the couch and stared at the TV someone had left on. The ear-deafening music drowned out the sound. It didn't matter. I would only have to stay another ten minutes.

Suddenly I felt the couch cushion tilt to the left; someone had sat down next to me. I turned to see who it was and was greeted by a blindingly white smile.

"How do you say 'great party' in Finnish?"

"*Hyvät bileet.*"

Greg tried to repeat the words, but he dropped the 'h' and the 't' and smushed the words together until it sounded more like "*yväbilee.*" I bit my lip to stop the laughter from escaping; it would only have encouraged him. He shook his head and laughed.

"Fuck it, I can't say it. I'll leave Finnish to you Finns, Finlandia is good enough for me. Cheers!"

I watched as he downed his drink. The thought came to me as he flashed yet another white smile in my direction. He may have been an American, but he was a handsome American and I hadn't had sex in months. I would never have to see him again.

He was the perfect one-night-stand.

· · · · · ● · · · ·

And he would have been the perfect one-night-stand if I had said goodbye the next morning the way I had planned.

I sip my coffee and wonder why I always change my plans and think something good is going to come out of it. All the warning signs were there, lined up like on a fucking Fourth of July parade on Main Street. I ignored all of them. If only I had listened to myself I wouldn't have left everything I knew behind.

But I didn't.

And of course I didn't. I was convinced love was worth any and all costs it extracted; it's what we're taught to believe from the moment we're old enough to walk.

I look up and notice a crack where the ceiling and wall connect. It looks as if it's been drawn with a pen. I know it's just an illusion created by shadows, but it looks real enough. Shadows trick the eyes and they're not the only things that trick us. There are so many things that trick us, and we allow ourselves to be tricked more than not, because we want to believe what we see and feel is real.

My feelings for Greg were real. I know they were, but I'm not so sure anything about him was real. There were so many things that didn't make sense. I remember telling myself I was misunderstanding him the first two months of our marriage. I had every reason for my suspicion as our general outlook on life couldn't have been more different. Finns rarely smile and they don't like to talk about their feelings. Americans are walking toothpaste commercials and they vent their feelings with a confidence possessed only by those who have never been told to shut up.

But it wasn't just that. His need to place himself in the middle of every occasion no matter how big or small was puzzling, as was his need to always be admired. No one does admirable things all the time. We do shitty things too. In fact, we do more shitty things than admirable things, so why would anyone need to hear how wonderful they are all the time? And why did he expect *me* to say *I* was sorry all the time?

And then he left.

Why did he leave? He said I didn't love him; that I thought only of myself. I had flown to the other side of the world to be with him and I didn't love him enough? The whole situation was like going out in -40°C/F weather with wet clothes on; the reality of the situation pierces your mind with the precision of a thousand frozen water molecules: he has been fucking with your mind and you let him.

"*Eikö se riitä jo?*" I ask myself.

I already know the answer. We're not done yet. We have to live apart for six months before one of us can apply for a divorce. It's like living with a ghost that is always there, right behind you. A menacing ghost that makes you cry until you can't breathe anymore.

I put my mug in the sink. I stare at the crack on the brim for a moment. I don't even know why I'm sad Greg's gone. Life with him wasn't what I thought it would be. And of course it wasn't. His love was just an illusion; an illusion only life could dispel and brutally so. I feel as if I have been thrashed and mangled by life for the past year.

I have no illusions left.

3

I leave the Mexican grocery store and cross the street. I switch my bag to my left shoulder. It feels heavy although I only bought a few items. I feel tired. I had to work overtime again. The flu has kept people home all week, although I doubt they're all sick. I suspect a few are using the flu as an excuse to take a few days off. It's hard to get days off here and vacations are pretty much non-existent. I can't say I blame them, but I hope I won't have to do this too many days in a row. Smiling for twelve hours is too much for me.

I see two young men eyeing me from the other side of the street. I tell myself there is nothing to fear although I'm still self-conscious of the fact that I'm one of the few light-skinned women in this neighborhood—except for the nuns who live a few blocks down the street, but they don't count. I suppose this is what it feels like to be an immigrant in Finland too. The newcomers are different in ways that make them stick out, although they are the same in all the ways that count. I wish I had been nicer to the ones I met, tried to make friends.

It's hard to be different and it's even harder to make friends when the only thing people see is that difference. I remember the summers I visited my dad in Sweden after my parents divorced and my mom moved back to Finland with me. I looked just like everyone else, but I sounded different. My dad wanted me to find new friends, but the only friend I found was Krista, a summer child from Lapland. She didn't snicker when I spoke and she didn't make me feel ashamed of where I was from. My dad kept on telling me I should try harder, but he seemed oblivious of all the reasons most girls didn't want to be friends with me.

Greg didn't understand either what I meant when I tried to explain why I feel I don't fit in here. He looks like me, but he doesn't stick out the way I do. I'm an immigrant with a weird accent and weird clothes. Everyone on our street knows who I am by now, but they don't talk to me. Maybe it's for the best since I don't know how to talk to them. Maybe I'm too honest, or maybe I say the wrong things, or maybe I do both. It always annoyed Greg, but he didn't do anything to help me. He just said, "You're in America now," as if it explained everything. I tried to tell him I knew where I was, but that I didn't understand how people talk. I still don't. It's not just the words people use. It's the *way* people talk. Words seem to mean nothing here, or maybe people are so used to hearing the same platitudes that no one pays any attention anymore. But why speak then? It makes no sense to speak if no one actually listens. But what makes sense anymore? I'm married, but I live alone. I live in a neighborhood where people eye me with suspicion. Even the police slow down when they drive by. Greg told me they think I'm here to buy drugs when I asked him about it. The thought makes me laugh even now. I can barely afford to live as is. How would I buy drugs? Besides, I wouldn't know what to buy, even if I had the money.

An elderly woman looks at me from her porch. I smile. She doesn't return the smile. She probably thinks I'm another gentrifier. That's what Greg said. I didn't know what he meant by it. I looked up the word and was even more confused. I don't have any money. I live here because it's where our apartment was when I arrived. I didn't choose it, Greg did. But I know I make people uncomfortable for some reason and I feel as if I should apologize, but I'm not sure what exactly I'm supposed to apologize for.

The thought of Greg reminds me he hasn't called or texted since he left. I don't even know where he is.

I stop and close my eyes for a moment.

I really need to stop lying to myself.

I know *exactly* where he is, just as I know why he wanted to live in this neighborhood, and it wasn't because the rent was cheap.

I open the front door. It almost hits my cat that has been waiting for me. It looks at me with eyes filled with accusation.

"*Anteeksi,* I'm sorry," I say and pet its furry head.

I get a pleased purr as a response.

My cat follows me to the kitchen and sits down by the fridge; its eyes follow my every move as I put the groceries away. I open a can of tuna for my cat and uncork a bottle of wine for myself. It's our evening routine: fish for the cat, wine for me. I feel as if I've been sucked into a vacuum.

It's the same thing every day.

"*Olisi kiva jos osaisit puhua*, but of course you can't talk," I say as I watch my cat eat its dinner.

I sigh.

I would be happy if I had someone to talk to just a few minutes a day, someone who actually cared. People here talk incessantly, but no one seems to care about the person they are talking to. They all talk about themselves and nothingness. Everything is always great and awesome, and everyone seems to think it's normal.

I think it's insane.

I sip my wine and look through the pile of mail on the counter. I read the address tab on the first letter. I want to throw it in the trash. My name isn't Maria, it's Marja; Marja Tuulevi Männynkoski to be precise. I wish I could change the "i" into a big fat red "j" and return it to the sender, but what good would it do? Americans can't make their r's hard and their tongues slip to the top to form an "i" instead of finding the bottom to form a "j." I tried to teach Greg how to say my name right. He made it sound more like Morja, and that was worse, so I resigned being called Maria. But it doesn't mean people shouldn't get it right when typing. Maybe it's the combination of two unpronounceable names that is the problem. Maybe if I had taken Greg's last name they would get my first name right.

Greg was furious when I refused to change my last name. I asked him why I should change my name just because I signed a marriage contract; no one changes their name when they buy a house or a car. In retrospect perhaps my refusal to take his last name caused Greg to think I didn't love him. He said it was an embarrassment to have a wife with a different last name. Or perhaps he didn't actually care if I loved him. He seemed to always care about what other people thought of him. My opinion of him didn't matter.

My cat licks its lips and walks past me.

"*Maistuiko se hyvältä?* Was it good?"

It doesn't acknowledge me.

Ungrateful animal.

Or maybe it isn't being ungrateful. Why should it thank me for doing my part of our agreement? I give it food and it keeps the rats away. That's what we agreed on.

If only people would keep their agreements too.

I think of the four and a half months I have to wait until I can file for a divorce. Sometimes I wish I could go back in time and undo all of it. But of course I can't; no one can. I just wish I hadn't fallen in love. I don't even know how it happened. I knew then, just as I know now, that it's impossible to fall in love with a perfect stranger. But I didn't think Greg was a stranger after the night we spent together. I thought we shared a deep connection—when I looked him in the eyes I saw myself. I should have known I was only looking at my own reflection.

I should have, but I didn't.

Instead I married him.

I close my eyes briefly. Why the *fuck* did I marry him? I have no explanation other than stupidity. I wanted to believe in our love story and I thought Greg believed in it too. I want to kick myself for thinking he meant it. Maybe I deserve to be here all alone. No, no one deserves to be this alone. Loneliness is like ice on bare skin; it hurts.

I swirl my wine and watch as it forms rivulets against the glass. I don't even know why I'm doing it. Air is not going to change the slightly bitter flavor of the wine that is cheaper than coffee.

Cheap.

I feel cheap. I have to be since it was so easy for Greg to throw me away. And maybe I am. I did sleep with him that first night. I guess he had no respect for me after that. But why did he marry me then? I asked him about it on our honeymoon. He told me he married me because I made him smile. His answer made no sense to me. And it made even less sense when I didn't make him smile anymore; quite the opposite. Just seeing me seemed to make him mad. Maybe that was the real reason he left.

I know I shouldn't blame Greg for everything. I answered the phone myself and got on that plane myself—twice. No one forced me. But of course I want to blame him. He didn't tell me everything.

He didn't tell me about Alene.

The thought of Alene fills my mind with rage and something I think is jealousy. Greg didn't tell me about his ex-wife before we got married. It wasn't until I saw them walking down the street as if they were a happy couple a few weeks after our wedding that I found out he had been married before. I asked Greg who she was when he got home. He began to yell at me, saying I didn't trust him, that I didn't love him, how they were just friends. That was the end of that conversation. It's how most of our conversations about Alene began and ended.

I know Alene is the reason Greg wanted to live here, in this neighborhood. He's with her now, I'm convinced of it. I don't have any proof of it, but I don't need any proof. Having lived a year in Alene's shadow I just know. Greg used to run to her like a puppy every time she called. And she called him more than she should have, more than anyone should have. Someone at church told me Alene left Greg having grown tired of his many flirtations. Maybe she regretted the divorce. I can't blame her for that, but I can blame her for not leaving him alone after he married me. Or maybe she doesn't know he married me, but how could she not? I know Greg stayed with her the first time he left. He told me about it when he came back two days later.

I know Greg and Alene are somewhere nearby although I haven't seen them. I guess Greg is avoiding this part of the neighborhood for obvious reasons. I know I shouldn't be thinking about them, but I can't help it. I think of Greg kissing Alene, touching her, smiling at her the way he used to smile at me and it's making me mad. I look up suddenly and nearly spill my wine. Why do I think I'm becoming mad? I *am* mad! I'm mad at both of them! But mostly I'm mad at myself. Why didn't I say goodbye that morning? I have no idea.

Or maybe I do.

It wasn't just that I thought I knew Greg. There was

something about the way he spoke. His voice was like a smooth river as he whispered words every woman wants to hear. But it was more than that. Greg was everything I wanted in a man. He was confident, sweet and kind. And he talked. He talked about his feelings, his dreams. It wasn't difficult to be captivated since Finnish men keep famously silent in two languages—unless they've had enough vodka, in which case you can't shut them up. And he lived in the moment and made me feel the present was a good place to be in. I wanted to stay in that present with him forever.

. . . .

I remember waking up to the sun's rays playing on my face. I could sense Greg's body next to me even before I could see him. I turned around and just stared at him for a moment. I knew I had to wake him, he had a plane to catch, but I didn't want to. As long as he was asleep, he would stay.

I got up and tiptoed to the bathroom. I brushed my teeth and scrubbed my face. I looked at myself in the mirror for a moment. The telltale signs of too much drinking were there, but I didn't look too terrible. My cheeks were glowing and my eyes looked brighter. Greg had told me I looked like a Nordic goddess sometime before the sun rose. I knew he was exaggerating, but I absorbed every word like someone who had been thirsty far too long and had finally been led to an oasis.

I found my old bathrobe on the floor, put it on, and went

back to the bedroom. Greg was sitting on the edge of the bed stark naked, his hair ruffled. He smiled when he saw me, pulled me to himself, opened my robe, and kissed my stomach. He looked at me with his dark, intense eyes.

"I have to go to the airport soon."

"I know."

"I'll call you as soon as I land in Chicago, okay?"

"Okay," I said and smiled.

. . . .

I shouldn't have answered when he called. It was probably the dumbest decision I've ever made.

No, that's not true.

Moving here was the dumbest decision I've ever made.

I wish I had stayed home.

I finish the first glass in one sweep. I feel my muscles relax and a brief euphoria fills my mind. I refill the glass and take it with me to the living room. I turn on Netflix and pick *Wallander*. I've noticed listening to something familiar helps alleviate homesickness, although sometimes it increases it.

Tonight is one of those nights.

Even before the names of the actors have flashed on the screen, hot tears begin to run down my cheeks. I cover my face with my hands.

I want to be home, *now*.

Not tomorrow or whenever I get to leave this place.

I want to be home *right now*.

I hit pause and stare at the frozen TV screen through the tears. I feel as if someone has hit the pause button on my life. I can't rewind and change the past, but I can't move on either. All I can do is sit here and wait for time to move. I don't have the patience for it. I don't think anyone does. It would be so easy to pack my things, head to the airport and just forget about everything. But that would probably be the most idiotic thing I could do. It would trap me in a marriage that exists only on paper and who knows what complications would arise from that kind of situation.

I wipe my eyes and walk to the window. I stare at the November sky. The old buildings fade against the expanding whiteness; only the dark barren trees are clearly visible. I watch as the sky turns into an ethereal violet. The street lights come on. The violet transforms slowly into a darker shade of purple until all light vanishes and the sky becomes completely black. The few remaining leaves on the trees glow under the street lights as if they were painted with gold.

I look at the vast sky above the city. I feel as if I'm a million miles away from home. Hope is supposed to be the last thing that leaves, but sometimes hope is like a skittish animal that runs away when no one is looking.

I have no hope left.

I go back to the couch and drink the last of the wine in one long gulp. I can feel the room begin to spin suddenly. I drank too much too quickly and forgot to eat.

I make my way to the bathroom with unsteady legs. I grab my toothbrush and nearly push it into my throat. I leave the toothbrush in the sink and stumble into the bedroom. I fall on the bed and close my eyes.

I see Greg's smiling face hovering above me.

I tell the face to fuck off.

Then darkness.

4

I drag myself to the bus stop.

My head hurts and I feel tired. I woke up again in the middle of the night and couldn't fall back asleep. I spent the rest of the night counting the days until I can go back home.

One hundred twenty-nine more days.

It feels like a prison sentence; a prison that exists only in my mind, but isn't any less real because of it.

I glance at my phone and look toward the horizon. The bus is late again. American movies seem to always begin with someone being late for work, but this isn't a movie. I will lose money if I'm late.

A man passes me. He spits on the ground and huffs. He turns to look at me, takes a few steps and turns to look at me again. He stares at me for a full minute before he steps into the empty lot next to the building. At least he didn't ask if I wanted to have sex with him.

I wasn't so lucky yesterday.

. . . .

I was waiting for the bus when a man stopped and asked if I wanted to party; shorthand for if I wanted to sleep with him. When I said I was married, the man laughed and said it's okay to fuck on the side. I looked away until the man gave up and continued to walk down the street.

I glanced after him.
Did he really think I would say yes?
Maybe he did.

. . . .

After another ten minutes the bus finally stops in front of me. I give the driver a quick smile as I press my card against the reader. The woman looks at me as if to ask, "What the hell are you doing here girl?"

I wonder the same.

I take a seat at the back; it's where I usually sit in the mornings. I'm glad the bus is nearly empty. It means I won't have to share a tight space with people who eat, listen to music, and talk on their phones as if no one else was around. The bus is like a community center here: it's a place for people to connect with friends and take care of business, and the louder the better. I've noticed Chicagoans like everything loud. People talk loudly, eat loudly, listen to music loudly, and no one seems to mind. I do, but I've learned to shut up and pretend I don't.

I notice a man on the other side of the aisle. He pours Butterfinger bites from a box right into his mouth and chews them looking extraordinarily pleased with himself. Sugar provides a cheap high. I tell myself I don't have any right to judge him. I look for the same high myself every day.

The bus rattles and shakes as if it's an old roller coaster made out of wood. The streets are in a terrible shape in this neighborhood. Perhaps the city will finally do something about them this coming year. Or maybe more white people will have to move into the area before it will happen. That's what Greg said when I complained. I didn't understand what he meant. Why wouldn't they pave the roads equally? Everyone pays taxes here. Isn't it how roads are paid for?

The bus is about to reach Western Avenue when a middle-aged woman gets up and begins to yell at a man on the other side of the aisle.

"I ain't stupid! This ain't Detroit! Did you hear me? I ain't *stupid* and this *ain't* Detroit!"

The man shakes his head and tries to ignore the woman. I glance at her. Either she is going home from a party or she has had something other than coffee for breakfast. I stopped being surprised months ago. It's easier to find liquor than groceries in this neighborhood. In Finland you have to go to the sparsely distributed government-owned ALKO, but this neighborhood has a church, liquor store, and a pharmacy on every block. It's as if the neighborhood is designed to provide a cure for every human ailment other than poverty.

I've said jokingly that I live two blocks from civilization. I should have said ten. Every month another business vanishes and the boarded-up doors and windows tell all about the abject poverty of Humboldt Park in a way the old regal buildings don't. On a warm summer's day the neighborhood looks almost prosperous and it's hard to differentiate it from the neighboring Wicker Park. But as soon as the cold weather returns, the cockiness of the lightly clad summer bodies gives way to the huddled emaciated creatures that are seen on every corner. I haven't told anyone at home what this neighborhood looks like.

They wouldn't believe me even if I did.

The bus stops at a traffic light. I watch as a cement worker parks the truck by his car and opens the trunk after three tries. He throws his jacket into the trunk with a tired movement. Perhaps he has had a long week or a lifetime of long weeks. Too much work wears people out. And still, the idea persists anyone can get ahead with hard work and most seem convinced they are the ones who will make it; they are the ones who will strike it rich. For most people the only thing that lay ahead is a broken body and disillusionment. I wonder again why people think they need to have lots of money to be happy. I would be happy if I had enough money to live well.

That's not true.

I used to have enough. It didn't make me happy. I complained about taxes and immigrants. I thought people were lazy and didn't want to work. I'm an immigrant now and I'm not lazy. Maybe the people who came to Finland weren't lazy either. Sometimes we have to go to the other side of the world to see the truth that was always right in front of us. But it doesn't mean I don't wish I had enough now. It's incredibly hard to be as poor as I am. My job pays me eleven hundred and fifty six dollars after taxes. My rent is eight hundred, leaving me three hundred fifty sixty dollars. After I pay utilities, I have two hundred and eighty dollars left. Transportation takes a hundred, leaving me hundred and eighty dollars for the rest.

That's forty-five dollars per week.

I know I'm not the only one struggling here. Money pools into the hands of the few instead of flowing freely and providing abundance for all like it should.

As if wanting to affirm my thoughts, the city changes before my eyes. The buildings become taller, the signs bigger, the storefronts glitzier. They advertise the opulent wealth of the core of the city. It's like arriving in a different world. A world no one from my neighborhood belongs in.

The thought reminds me how I felt I didn't belong in Greg's world either. It was as if I was only visiting instead of being a permanent part of his life. But why am I thinking about him again? Why can't I just forget him?

I thought I saw Greg yesterday, but it wasn't him. It was just another stranger in a city filled with strangers. I wiped a tear off my cheek and told myself to stop being stupid. Even if it had been him, did I really think he would have wanted to talk to me? I feel like such a fool for continuing to believe love is the solution to all of life's problems. Why do I think it is?

I know why.

. . . .

I was sixteen when I became hooked on the idea love was going to make everything all right.

I was on my way to Sweden to spend the summer with my dad. I went up to the deck to watch the ship leave Turku. After a few minutes I noticed a young man with blond curly hair standing a couple of meters from me by the railing. I glanced at him a couple of times. He must have noticed I was looking at him because he smiled and said hello.

It was all it took.

. . . .

I didn't hear back from Magnus after that summer. He promised he would call, but never did. Maybe that's why I was so eager to answer the phone when Greg called. I wanted to fix the past and not let another one slip away.

How dumb of me.

You can't fix the past with new mistakes. And yet I tried and not just because of Magnus.

It had everything to do with Antero too.

. . . .

I met Antero when I was twenty-one. He was the quintessential Finn in every way with his straw-colored hair and pale complexion. He would never have talked to me and I would certainly never have looked at him twice if it hadn't been for the fact that he rescued me from getting swallowed up by a swamp.

Sara and I had made a New Year's resolution to begin a healthier lifestyle. The previous year we had decided to give up candy; it ended by Easter. And because it did, I wasn't prepared when on a cold June afternoon Sara announced suddenly we were going on a hiking trip. I wondered why she wanted to become a walking food supply for mosquitos. I certainly didn't. But I knew Sara wouldn't relent, so I packed my backpack, hopped on the bus, and hoped it would get a mechanical failure all the way to Kuusamo.

Our group took off the next morning. After a couple hours I had to stop to adjust my backpack. I told Sara, but maybe she didn't hear me, because fifteen minutes later I found myself all alone in the middle of the forest.

Our group had vanished.

I ran in the direction I thought everyone had gone and ended up ankle-deep in a swamp. The more I tried to move, the more I sank.

After a few panicked minutes, I heard a voice behind me. *"Älä liiku."*

I stopped moving and stood absolutely still as Antero grabbed branches from nearby pine trees and spread them around my feet. He told me to lift my left foot carefully while he helped me balance my weight. I heard a sound as if a suction cup had been pulled off a window as my foot became free. I lost my balance for a second and fell right into Antero's waiting arms. Something happened that moment, something I still can't explain. I never thought it was possible, but swamp water cemented us together.

Then one day he vanished from my life.

· · · · ·•· · · · ·

I still don't know what happened. We were talking about moving in together. We had our whole lives mapped out. Then one day, out of the blue, Antero sent me a text and said he was sorry, but he couldn't do it. He had to break up with me.

That's it.

I called and texted him at least a hundred times, but he didn't answer. After a week I stopped. I drank a whole bottle of vodka while I cried and cursed till I lost my voice. When I woke up the next morning I decided I was never going to love again. I was going to spend the rest of my life alone. I didn't leave my apartment for anything other than work for weeks. I didn't want to see or talk to anyone. Sara was getting exasperated with me, but I didn't see any point with life anymore.

Then I met Greg.

Maybe I didn't move to Chicago to be with Greg as much as I wanted to get away from Antero's memory. Maybe Greg felt it. Maybe that's why he kept on saying I didn't love him. Maybe I lied to him as much as he lied to me.

That's not true.

I may have wanted to get away from the memories, but I still came here to be with him. I did love him, no matter how many times he told me I didn't. *He* was the one who left me to wait for an end that is months away.

One hundred twenty-nine more days.

I feel I'm being punished, but I don't know why.

All I did was love.

5

The bus stops at a red light.

The driver glances at the rearview mirror.

"Hey, you!"

A young man looks at the driver and points at himself as if to ask if the driver is talking to him.

"No, not you, the man behind you, the one with the open beer container. Hey man, you can't drink beer on the bus! You need to get off now!"

The man looks out the window and ignores the driver.

"Did you hear me? You need to get off now or I'll call the police and they'll take you to jail!"

The man turns and gives the driver a look that is both defiant and bored.

"Just let me off at the stop. I've paid my fare."

"No, you need to get off now!"

The man shakes his head and gets up. I stare at the floor as he passes me. At least he didn't get mad and start threatening the driver. Chicagoans are aggressive in a way that makes them unpredictable, at least to me. I never know if it's just the way they talk or if they are about to lose it.

I glance at the driver. She stares at the man as he leaves the bus. She shakes her head and brushes her braids of her shoulder as she turns to look at the traffic.

I wouldn't want to have the driver's job.

I wouldn't know what to do.

I get off the bus at Michigan Avenue.

A man stops and asks for a cigarette. I tell him I don't smoke and continue to walk. The man runs after me and asks if I have fifty cents. I shake my head. I've learned to leave all change at home. That way I can say I have no money and it won't be a lie.

The man turns around and continues to walk down the street looking for someone who has a cigarette or fifty cents to give him. Sometimes I wonder if every person who begs is really in need. It would mean poverty in this city is so widespread people must constantly accost every person they meet to ensure they get what they need.

Perhaps it's true.

The staggering difference between those who have enough and those who don't is so glaringly obvious in this city. But I've noticed people here don't want to see the actual face of poverty although no one can avoid it entirely. Beggars can't be hidden no matter how often they are told to move on. Chicago is big and impressive, much bigger than any city in Finland, but it's just a façade that tries to hide the ugly reality that is right in front of everyone. In my opinion a city is only as impressive as its ability to take care of its people. Finland may be smaller in every way, but at least people don't have to make the street their permanent home, unless they want to. I tried to explain it to Greg, why I thought the system here is unjust. He told me I should be glad I got to live in a free country.

I didn't bring it up again.

I reach the mall and enter the bright building.

I remember the first time I walked through the revolving doors. It felt as if I had walked into an ancient Roman bath that had been converted into a Parisian catwalk. I looked at the people who walked aimlessly from store to store wearing their expensive designer clothes. It was as if they had arrived to a party that was cancelled. There was no celebration, only an endless search for the high that wore off a long time ago.

I walk quickly to the bathroom; I drank too much coffee to wake myself up this morning. I see a woman brushing her hair in front of the mirror. Her entire being says retail. Endless people-pleasing leaves its indelible mark on people's faces and bodies. Money leaves its mark too. Wealthy women have stiffer necks and colder eyes; they don't seek to please anyone. They are a bit like Finns, except people in Finland have the same demeanor without the money and their manners aren't as smooth. Greg used to complain I was too direct, that I didn't know how to be tactful. I listened as he said all the right things for all the wrong reasons and wondered why he thought lying to people was any better.

I take my place behind the cash register. I see Jimena helping a customer by one of the displays. She smiles and waves at me.

I return the smile.

Jimena transferred to our store a few days ago. I'm glad she did. She's the only one who is friendly and talks to me.

"*¡Hola, cariño!* How was your day off?" asks Jimena, leaning against the counter.

"It was okay."

"Only okay?! *Ay,* Marja! I wish you had called me! My cousin threw a party yesterday. She's a bit *extraña*, but she knows how to throw parties like no one else. Let me show you a picture!"

Jimena pulls her phone from her pocket. We aren't allowed to have our phones with us on the store floor, but Jimena said it was a lot of nonsense when I mentioned it. She said we need to entertain ourselves somehow when business is slow

"*Mira*, look! We had so much fun!"

I glance at the photo.

"You should become a model," I say and smile.

"Nah, I don't think so."

"No, I mean it, you should. You know how to pose."

"You mean like this?"

Jimena purses her lips and brushes her hair aside. I shake my head and laugh. Jimena is as irreverent as she is beautiful. There is no fear in her eyes; they glimmer as she speaks. No wonder men like her. She's like the northern lights against the dark sky—magnetic and luminous.

I'm more like a spring flower everyone gets excited about when it appears in early spring, but is quickly forgotten when the colorful summer flowers arrive. There's nothing noteworthy about me; although I've noticed American men find me attractive for some reason. Jimena said I'm cute when I wondered about it out loud after yet another customer asked for my phone number. Cute isn't a compliment, not from someone like Jimena, but I know she means well.

An elderly woman with ill-fitting clothes and an outdated hairdo stops in front of us; she has come to let Jimena take her break. She gives me a brief smile as she takes her place behind the register. I glance at the woman. She has the air of importance most people who work in high-end retail gain after a while. It's the perfect merging of the person selling the product and the product being sold. I wonder why she feels so important working here. I guess it's because she's so close to money she can smell it, but not close enough to actually have any. She reminds me of Mrs. Bucket from the old English TV-show. The thought makes me laugh out loud. The woman gives me a withering glare. I bite my lower lip and stare at the register. I forgot to appear serious while smiling. It's such a strange combination I'm still not sure how the two are supposed to go together.

I glance at the woman while she talks to a customer. Her voice is high-pitched and syrupy, her smile exaggerated. She reminds me of all the women I met at church. It was as if the church had turned all of them into Barbies. All they cared about was their looks and homes, and how to get Ken to marry them as quickly as possible if they happened to be single. I felt as if I had arrived from the moon; or maybe I had gone to the moon myself. There was nothing normal about the way they behaved.

I didn't like going to church, but Greg thought it was the greatest thing ever. I never could understand why he was so excited. It wasn't as if he ever lived what they preached.

Then I met the reason.

Her name was Candy.

Americans give such strange names to their children, especially girls. When Candy introduced herself to me after a church service I nearly chocked. I tried to imagine a Finnish child running on the school ground, being called Karkki. The thought was so impossible it still makes me laugh. But I don't laugh when I think of Candy. She was after Greg the moment she saw him and Greg was like a piranha in an aquarium; he circled her as if he was ready to devour her. He found every excuse to talk to her and he sent playful messages throughout the day—until someone got whiff of it and put a stop to it. How that happened wasn't so difficult to understand. The church policed sexual sins as if KGB had provided the training. There would be no unlawful sexual unions in the church, thank you very much.

Did Candy have anything to do with why Greg left? I doubt it. He got bored with her, especially after he knew he was being watched. I guess he got bored with me too. The only person he didn't ever seem to get bored with was Alene. Why he didn't have the sense to stay away from other women while he was married to her was something I could never understand. But very few things about Greg made any sense.

Jimena returns from her break and the elderly woman gets ready to leave, but not before giving me another disapproving glance.

Jimena looks at me and frowns.

"What happened?"

"I don't know. I guess she doesn't like me."

"Don't worry, she doesn't like anybody. I bet she doesn't even like herself."

I smile and turn to greet the next customer. Jimena has the ability to make me smile even when there isn't much to smile about. And I know Jimena's right, but it hurts nevertheless. It's strange how the disapproval of strangers can cause so much pain. We shouldn't care, but we do. The only person who doesn't care what other people think of her is Jimena. I know I should become more like her, but I'm not sure I have it in me. I don't think any Finn does. Bravery before strangers isn't something we do.

Jimena looks at her phone. She giggles as she reads a text. She types a quick response, puts her phone away, and asks if I want to go out sometime this week. I think about the forty-five dollars I have to spend this week. I say sure, but only if it doesn't cost too much. Jimena smiles and says *por supuesto*. She doesn't have any extra money either. We may live different lives in many ways, but the lack of money unites us. Poverty is the one thing that doesn't discriminate.

Not even here.

6

I open the door and enter the dimly lit room. I see Jimena sitting by the bar. She is wearing a glitzy pink halter top and her long black hair cascades down her back. I touch my ponytail instinctively. I feel plain and dull, and compared to Jimena I know I am.

"Hi," I say and sit down on the chair next to Jimena. She raises her left index finger to indicate she needs a moment; she is waiting for a text. I notice Jimena is drinking beer. I order one for myself. Jimena finishes typing, puts her phone down, and gives me a bright smile.

"*¡Hola!* Carlos says hi."

"You told your husband about me?" I ask with wide eyes.

"Of course! I tell him everything."

I take a sip of my beer and think how nice it must be to be married to someone who actually cares and is kind. I thought Greg was caring and kind too, but in the end he turned out to be anything but kind.

"Forget about your husband. You'll find someone new."

I glance at Jimena. I forget sometimes she can read me like an open book.

"I don't know if I want to," I say quietly.

"But of course you do! One bad relationship isn't the end. You'll find love again."

"Maybe. I just don't know why love has to be so difficult."

"*Si, amor es dificil*, but without love there's no life."

I want to say she's wrong. But then again, maybe she isn't. Maybe love isn't the problem, maybe I'm the problem. Maybe I just don't know how to choose the right person. I know anyone can say "I love you" and that it can be a truth, a half-truth, or a complete lie. I just don't ever seem to know which one it is before it's too late. Maybe it's because I expect people to tell the truth; it's what Finns are taught to do. The press doesn't lie and politicians know how to stay honest at the risk of losing their cushy positions. But men seem to be another story altogether.

I glance at Jimena. She's staring at her phone again. I don't mind. We don't need to talk. It feels good to just spend time with someone. Besides, I mostly just listen to Jimena anyway. She loves to talk and I have a hard time coming up with things to say, although I've noticed she has the ability to get me to talk about things I'd rather not.

I told Jimena almost the whole story. I left out the fact that I slept with Greg the first night. It made me feel like a slut, although Jimena wouldn't have seen it that way. She said once sex is like food; why starve yourself if you don't have to? I left other parts out too. I didn't tell her about the way Greg made me feel I should be grateful for being allowed to stay, that he threatened me with divorce and deportation if I didn't do as he said. Maybe that's why he left me so I would be kicked out of the country. Or maybe he's just a lying piece of shit who brought me here to make his ex-wife jealous. I don't know what the truth is anymore.

I don't think even Greg knows.

I take a sip of my beer and smile to myself. For a moment I feel almost like myself, the way I used to feel before I came here. I know it's because of Jimena; she's good company. I don't have to pretend when I'm with her, not the way I had to with Greg and everyone else. I feel as if Jimena is my first real friend here.

I had lots of "friends" in the beginning. Everyone at our church wanted to make me feel welcomed once they heard I was from overseas. I shouldn't have been surprised when I didn't hear from them again after I stopped attending. I always got the feeling they liked me only when I behaved in a certain way.

I know Jimena goes to Mass every morning. She said she goes because someone has to drive *Abuela* Rosalita and she's the only one who has the time to take her. She doesn't believe most of the things she hears, although she did confess she occasionally prays her husband will finally get his papers. They married more than a year ago in Guadalajara, but he can't come here, not yet. I've heard Jimena joke she became a widow the day she got married. The shadow that passed her face told me it wasn't exactly a joke.

I came here with a fiancé visa. It was expensive, but easy. Jimena's husband can't come here yet no matter how much money they spend. They married outside of the country and that means they have to wait two years. Jimena told me she didn't realize her mistake before it was too late. But she's also afraid immigration officials won't believe their story. Jimena's husband is from Mexico and he must therefore be after a Green Card. That Jimena is gorgeous and any man would be so lucky to be with her doesn't play into the equation. He must want to come here, because America is the greatest country in the world, the one place where everyone has the same opportunity.

So they say.

Everyone knows it's a lie.

But it's a lie too that no one can make it. Jimena's family came here three generations ago and they have been thriving. Nothing is cut and dried when it comes to immigration, not even in the wealthiest country in the world.

Jimena orders another beer and shows me a picture.

"What do you think of this dress? It's nice, yes?"

"Yes, it's nice."

"I can't wait to show it to Carlos."

"When are you going to see him?

"Hopefully after Christmas. He should be getting his papers soon."

"What does he think about moving here?"

"He says it's an imperialistic hellhole," says Jimena laughing.

I look at Jimena with wide eyes.

"Oh, he just has all these weird political ideas."

"What are you going to do if he doesn't like living here?"

"Then we'll move to Mexico," says Jimena, shrugging.

I glance at Jimena. She made it sound as if living in another country is just as easy as being home.

It isn't.

Most people don't think about the difference when they make plans; I know I didn't. They leave their homes hoping for a better future only to end up looking back, hoping to return. I know I'm lucky I *can* return. Finland isn't a war-torn country or plagued by famines. What do people who can't return do? They say, "Next year in Havana." It's consoling and depressing at the same time. Consoling, because you know you're safe; depressing, because you live in a country where not everyone wants you. It's like being bullied in school: you don't need the whole class to bully you to feel you're not accepted.

I finish my beer and order another. I can afford three beers, I count. After that I'll have to stop drinking. It's not a bad thing. I don't want to take the CTA while drunk. You never know what can happen.

"You know, you should go on a date," says Jimena suddenly.

"I don't think so," I say, shaking my head.

"Oh, come on! It'll do you good!"

"Don't you think I should get divorced first?"

"It's just a pick me up, you know, to make you feel good."

I stare at Jimena for a full minute. Feel good? How will spending time with a stranger make me feel good? Slowly the thought enters my mind as if through a dense fog.

Sex.

She means sex.

"Where would I find someone to go out with?"

"We're in a bar," says Jimena slowly.

I glance around the room. I shake my head to tell her I can't see anyone I'm interested in. Jimena makes a disapproving sound with her tongue. I know what that means. She's annoyed. I don't want to upset her. Jimena is my only friend here.

"Maybe I should try online dating," I say, laughing mildly.

"*Ay, cariño,* what a *fantastic* idea!"

I stare at Jimena's beaming face and wonder what the hell I've gotten myself into this time.

I get out of the car and wave at Jimena. She insisted on paying for the ride. I felt ashamed, because I couldn't pay half of it. Jimena just smiled and said it was okay.

I unlock the door and walk straight to the kitchen. I pour myself a glass of wine. I forgot to eat again and the beer made me nauseous. I hope the wine will settle my stomach.

I take the glass to the living room and turn on Netflix. I choose a movie and regret my choice almost instantly. The actors use fuck as a period, comma, and exclamation mark, and they seem to only be interested in sex.

The thought of sex reminds me I have now a Tinder account thanks to Jimena. I told her it was a bad idea, but she just laughed and told me to live a little. I'm supposed to report back to her when I find a date. Maybe I can just say I haven't found anyone and not even try. But I already know it won't work. She'll know.

She always does.

I click back to the first screen and scroll through the movies to find a new one. I don't want to watch anything happy but I can't deal with anything sad either. What else is there? Nature documentaries, I suppose. But even animals can look happy or sad. *You're being ridiculous*, I tell myself. And I know I am. Why did I have to suggest online dating of all things? I'm not ready to date, not by a long shot. You can't just walk away from a relationship and expect all feelings to go away on their own. You have to erase every damn memory that still makes you cry, every memory that still ties you to the past.

. . . .

I remember landing in New York two weeks before our wedding. My stomach was in knots and my head felt lighter than a helium balloon. I stood in a cramped room waiting to get a stamp that would allow me to board my connecting flight to Chicago. I listened to the immigration official tell me I had ninety days to get married or they would send me back home.

It sounded like such a terrible threat then.

. . . .

It wasn't, not really. I got married and they're going to send me home anyway unless I leave voluntarily. The thought reminds me I don't have enough money to pay for a plane ticket. I can't stay and I can't afford to leave. It would be hilarious if it wasn't so tragic.

My phone beeps.

I glance at the screen and sit up straight.

I feel as if someone has struck me with a paddle and I've landed in cold water.

It's Greg.

He wants to come over.

7

I open my eyes slowly.

My head hurts and my mouth feels dry.

I get up and walk slowly to the bathroom. I look at myself in the mirror. I look like hell. I think about taking a shower, but what's the point? It's my day off and I have nowhere to go. What does it matter what I look like?

I go to the kitchen.

I see a mug on the counter next to the coffee maker. It's Greg's favorite mug. He drank from it last night. The mug is still in the kitchen, but Greg isn't, and I know why.

Ex sex.

It was all he was after and I fell for it, hook, line, and sinker.

Vitun idiootti!

Why did I tell him to come over? Why didn't I just tell him to fuck off? I have a faint memory of Greg arriving after midnight. He smiled the way he did that first morning when he told me he wanted to see me again. A few moments later we were on the couch, kissing as if time was going to end soon.

I wish it had.

I drink a glass of water and feed my cat. I return to the bedroom and crawl back to bed. I can still smell Greg on the sheets. It's a scent that used to make me wild.

It still does.

I can still feel his hands on my body. I can feel him kissing me deeply, just like he used to. I can feel his weight on me as he pinned my arms under his hands, how he was inside me with one sharp movement.

Lopeta jo! Stop!

I close my eyes. Jimena is right. I need to fuck someone until my body no longer remembers him, until it no longer wants him. I grab my phone from the nightstand. I click on the Tinder app and I swipe through the pictures. Suddenly the app stops working.

"Mitä helvettiä? What the fuck!" I say out loud, looking at the phone. The popup tells me I have maxed out my swipes for the day. I can pay $19.90 for an upgrade or wait till the next day.

Tears of self-pity fill my eyes. I can't even find a fuckbuddy without screwing things up! I put my phone back on the nightstand and pull the blanket over my head.

I just want to forget about everything.

I wake up and look at my phone.

It's almost six. I've slept all day.

Great.

Now I won't be able to sleep all night and I have to go to work tomorrow. At least my head doesn't hurt anymore.

That's something.

My cat jumps on the bed and looks at me with serious eyes as if it knows something is amiss. I smile at my cat and stroke its back. It rewards my strokes with soft purring. I wish my life was as easy as my cat's. All a cat has to do is eat, sleep, and play. It has no real problems, other than being hungry when I forget to feed it. As if it has read my thoughts, my cat meows.

"Yeah, I know, let's go."

I throw the blanket to the side, pick my cat up, and go to the kitchen.

I open a can of cat food and watch as my cat begins to eat eagerly. I think about making dinner for myself when the doorbell rings. I glance at the direction of the living room and wonder who it could be. The gate is locked; no one can come to the door—unless one of my neighbors has left the gate open again to let one of their friends in.

I sigh and walk to the front door ready to say "no thanks" to whoever is standing on the other side.

I open the door and see Greg's smiling face.

I stare at him for a moment.

"What are you doing here?" I say with a stunned voice.

"What do you mean? I told you I was coming at six. I mean, I know I'm late. Someone threw a fit on the bus and we had to wait for the cops to arrive. Do you really want me to go just because I'm a few minutes late?"

The accusation and hurt in his eyes make him look like a little boy. For a few seconds I try to remember hearing him say he would be back tonight.

I can't recall it.

I move aside and let Greg in. He sits down on the couch and turns on the TV.

"I thought you said you would have dinner ready," he says without looking at me. I stare at him and think of something to say. I can't think of anything.

I turn around and go to the kitchen.

I open the fridge and pull out the fresh tortellini I had saved for today. At least I had that. Greg wouldn't eat the food I usually eat.

I fill a pot with water and wait for it to come to a boil. I add the pasta to the roiling water and try to remember what we talked about last night. I have no memory of any of it.

Greg comes to the kitchen and looks into the fridge. I know he's looking for beer. I don't have any. I glance at him. I still don't know why he's here and it's making me nervous.

"What happened last night?" I ask, turning around.

"What do you mean by 'what happened last night'? You know what happened," says Greg, laughing.

I take a deep breath and try to keep my voice calm.

"No, I don't."

"Is this a joke?"

"No, it isn't. What happened?"

Greg laughs again and looks away for a moment.

"Okay, so we made love and you begged me to stay. That's what happened last night."

Suddenly the memories come rushing in like waters from a broken damn. I remember telling Greg how much I loved him, how I couldn't live without him, how I would do anything to make him stay. I remember begging, pleading, promising things, until he said he would stay. The humiliation of the situation is becoming acute in my mind.

Vitun viini!

The damned wine made me say things I had no intention of saying.

"I think the pasta is ready," says Greg and goes back to the living room.

I look at the tortellini.

The filling is bursting out of the overcooked pasta circles. It's the perfect replica of my own feelings. I feel as if I'm about to burst too. Why the hell did I ask Greg to stay?

But better yet, why did *he* agree to stay?

8

I get up and go to the bathroom. I step on the underwear Greg left on the floor last night. I pick them up and put them in the hamper. He is still just as much of a slob as he ever was. Other than that he's being nice—too nice. He's acting the way he did when we got married and it's making me nervous. I'm not sure why he's back or what he wants. He told me last night he left because he thought I didn't love him, but that he knows now that I do. I wonder what I said this time that convinced him since I failed all other times.

I turn on the shower and let the warm water cascade down my back. I wash my hair and soap my body. I grab the razor and begin to shave my legs. Greg dislikes hair on my body. He says it makes me unfeminine. Everything seems to make me unfeminine. I don't even know what feminine means—other than that it's everything I'm not. I push the razor too hard against my skin around my ankle. I wince as the water flushes against the cut. I really shouldn't shave during winter. My skin is too fragile for it. But I know if I don't, I'll get an irate lecture from Greg. He may be acting nice, but he's not that nice.

He never was.

I turn off the water and wrap my wet hair in a towel. I look at myself in the mirror. Something about the way the towel curls just above my forehead reminds me of the first morning. I remember smiling then.

I don't smile now.

We all think love is going to stay the same.

It doesn't.

I put on a clean T-shirt and go back to the bedroom. I see Greg putting on his socks with a hurried movement.

"Where are you going?"

"Alene called."

"So?"

"She needs my help."

"Do you have to?"

"What?"

"Go see her."

"Oh, come on, don't be that way! You know she can't lift heavy things."

I want to tell him I don't know anything about Alene, but it would be pointless. It would only lead to an argument.

Greg gets up and tries to kiss me. I turn my head away. He lets out a frustrated sigh.

"Look, I'll come back around eight, okay?"

I stare at the wall. What does he expect me to say? That I think it's okay I have to share his time with his ex-wife, that I know I share him in other ways too.

I hear the front door slam shut.

I turn to look at the bed for a moment.

"Voi saatana! Miksi mä luotin suhun!" I scream and pull the sheet from the bed with an angry movement. I collapse on the floor with the sheet in my hand. Large tears fall on

the purple fabric leaving dark spots behind.

It's hopeless.

It's all completely hopeless.

I sit on the floor and stare into nothingness. Why did I think things would be different this time? Greg is always going to come to me when he needs me, but he's never going to be there when I need him.

He's never going to change.

My phone rings.

I wipe my eyes, get up, and grab my phone from the nightstand.

"This is Marja... Hi, Jimena... You want to go to park? Isn't it cold? ... Yeah, you're right, the sun is out. ... In an hour? Okay, I'll see you there."

I put my phone back on the nightstand and wipe my eyes. I'm not so sure going to the park in November is such a great idea, but I guess it's better to spend the day with Jimena than crying alone.

I get off the train and take the escalator up to street level. I see Jimena waiting for me by the crosswalk. She grabs my arm and tells me how much fun we'll be having all day. I laugh at her enthusiasm. She's the only one I know who goes to the Millennium Park in November and acts as if it's in the middle of the summer.

We walk along the nearly deserted streets. It's the only good thing about cold weather: there are fewer tourists blocking all the streets with their endless meandering. The few who have decided to brave the weather take pictures and smile. They seem to think Chicago is beautiful city even when all the green is gone and only metal and asphalt remains. And of course they do. Every city looks beautiful to the untrained eye. I didn't see any of the flaws either when I came here the first time.

I only saw what I wanted to see.

We cross the street and walk to the Bean. It looks as if it has been taken hostage by the small crowd. I look at the people who smile and take selfies. They remind me of the time Greg brought me here when I came to visit him for the first time. It was in the middle of February and the frigid temperature had sucked all moisture from the air. I remember trying to get my hair to settle, but no matter what I did, I looked as if I had touched one of those magnetic balls that make your hair stick out. Greg just laughed, put his hands on both sides of my head to keep my hair still and told me it's why hats exist.

"So, did you find a date yet?" asks Jimena with a conspiratory smile.

I stare at the metal structure for a few seconds. I don't know how to say it, but I know I have to tell Jimena the truth.

"Greg's back," I say quietly.

I wait for Jimena to say something, but she remains silent—too silent. I notice her jaw is clenched and her eyes seem fixated at something in the distance. After a moment she turns to look at me.

"Why did he come back?"

"I'm not sure," I say, evading her eyes.

"It has something to do with his ex-wife, doesn't it?"

"I don't know."

"He's with her right now, isn't he?"

"Yeah," I say with a voice barely louder than a whisper.

Jimena throws her arms up in the air.

"Oh, my *God*, Maria! Aren't you upset? He didn't tell you about his ex-wife before you two got married. He left, came back, left again, came back, and now he's spending the whole day with her *again!*"

I look at Jimena. She called me Maria, although she knows how to say my name right. It means she's angry. I want to tell her exactly what I think, but there's nothing I can say that will make any sense.

"Listen," she says, grabbing my arm firmly. "You need to end it. He's using you."

"If I end it, they will send me home."

Jimena lets go off my arm as if she's been zapped. I can tell she's never considered that I could be sent home. Few know about the conditional residency requirement that will send me home if I get divorced before our second anniversary.

I turn my head and watch as two birds take flight from a nearby tree. They circle above us before they disappear behind the tall buildings. I look at the city's silhouette against the bright sky. The high-risers look like enormous sticks that reach toward the cloudy heavens leaving the dirt and grime behind. The thought of birds and dirt reminds me of the day I saw a gun violence victim just after Greg had left.

. . . .

I was almost home when I saw a group of people by a body; they were talking quietly amongst themselves. I could hear the piercing sound of sirens several blocks away. I watched as blood inched away from the lifeless body like warm molasses and seeped slowly into the dirty asphalt turning it dark red. I felt a wave of nausea flush over me. I didn't want to look at the body anymore. I raised my eyes and spotted a flock of birds flying across the cloudless sky. I wished I could fly away too, but I knew I couldn't. The young man hadn't been able to leave either and now he was dead.

The lyrics of Hotel California ran through my head as if someone had turned on a radio only I could hear.

Welcome to Chicago.

Such an awful place.

. . . .

I glance at the high-risers again. I don't even know why I'm upset. There's nothing for me here other than sorrow and sadness.

I turn to look at Jimena.

"You're right, I need to end it. And I don't mind, I want to go home."

Jimena squeezes my arm. She doesn't need to say anything. I know she understands. She thought I had gone mad when I told her about my life in Finland. She couldn't believe I left a country where people don't have to worry about getting old or sick. "The happiest country in the world!" she said, showing me the latest United Nations report. I tried to tell her about the xenophobia and the general gloominess during winter, but she just looked around and shrugged as if to say, "What's the difference?" I laughed and shook my head. Jimena is the only person I know who can make a point without words.

I will miss her.

9

I glance at my phone.

It's almost seven and there's no sign of Greg yet. He didn't come home last night. He didn't even call. I guess Alene wanted something more than just help with her furniture—if that was even the reason she asked him to come over in the first place.

I pause the movie and walk to the window. I look at the sky. The glow from the city hides most of the stars here. Only a lonely star twinkles in the vast space. I see a woman pushing a stroller on the other side of the street. Greg didn't want children. He told me so on our honeymoon. It was just another thing he hid from me. But I guess it was my fault too for not asking before we got married. I just assumed he did. All I can think is how glad I am now. The thought of having to stay here for eighteen years, struggling to survive on minimum wage without adequate healthcare and affordable child care makes my heart grow cold.

I sit back down on the couch and unpause the movie. Mindless staring dulls the mind and it's exactly what I need right now. If I think too much I won't be able to say what I need to.

I hear Greg opening the front door just as the movie ends.

I watch as he walks to the kitchen without looking at me. I can tell he's upset about something.

A few minutes later he comes back to the living room. He stops in front of me.

"Why are you on Tinder?"

I look away.

"I asked you a question!" he says with a harsh voice.

"My friend thought I needed to go on a date."

"A date!? What the hell were you thinking? You're a married woman!"

"Well, you weren't here. And how do you know I'm on Tinder?"

His cheeks flush and he looks uncertain for a moment. We both know the only way he can know about it is if he's there himself. He can't access my phone now that I've changed my password. He used to read my e-mails and personal messages regularly. He was sure I was cheating and he wanted to find the evidence. He seems to think he has found it now, but for some reason he seems oblivious of the fact that it makes him look equally guilty.

"I want you to leave," I say quietly.

Greg stares at me with wide eyes.

"Are you serious? You want *me* to leave? Have you forgotten they will send you home if we get divorced now?"

"No, I haven't."

"So you want to go back to that… that *hole* I found you in two years ago?"

I stare at the screen in silence. Greg's face becomes pale;

then it turns bright red. I can see his hands form into fists. I seem to be the only one who can bring the violence that is simmering just underneath the surface to the forefront. He's never hit me, but he always looks like he will.

"Goddammit, I *knew* you wouldn't know how to be an American! I should never have married you! You were a *complete* waste of my time!"

Greg walks to the front door, opens it with a swing, and slams it shut behind him. I can feel the tremor of the slammed door; my heart pounds as if it wants to come out. Slowly my body begins to relax. I lie down on the couch, pull my feet up, and curl up into a fetal position. I feel like a balloon that has been deflated without warning. I think about crying, but my eyes remain dry. A deep sense of relief flushes over me like a giant wave.

I did it.

It's over.

It's finally over.

10

A loud sound wakes me.

I sit up and look around the bedroom. For one disoriented moment I wonder where Greg is. I almost laugh out loud when I remember he's gone. I lie back down and close my eyes. Another wave of relief flushes over me. It's followed by a bout of sadness. I know I'm not sad because Greg's gone. I'm sad because my dream is gone, my beautiful dream that turned into a nightmare. The nightmare is gone too.

That's the reason for the relief.

My cat comes into the bedroom and jumps up on the bed. It looks around the room.

"He's not here," I tell my cat.

We look at each other for a moment. I grab my cat and hug it. It meows and struggles to get free.

"I know how you feel. It's like you're suffocating. It's how I used to feel too," I say and put my cat back down on the bed. It gives me an annoyed look, jumps off the bed, and runs back to the living room.

"I should have run away too, a long time ago," I say quietly to myself.

I get up and go to the bathroom. I brush my teeth and think how strange it feels to be single again. I'll have to get used to saying "me" instead of "we." I don't think it's going to be a problem. With Greg there never really was an "us." Everything was always about him. He would claim to do something just for me, but he never asked if I actually wanted to do the things he had planned. I learned quickly to pretend I had a good time, although I rarely did. It was easy in the beginning, but got harder as time passed. And I know I'm not exactly single yet. I'm still married, although I doubt Greg will come back this time. I know I hurt his pride when I asked him to leave.

I hear my phone beeping in the bedroom. I rinse my mouth quickly. I hope it's not Greg. He sent me an angry email in the middle of the night telling me I didn't deserve him, how he was glad I was out of his life. I deleted it. In four months one of us can file for a divorce. Maybe he's counting the days.

I know I am.

I look at my phone. It's Jimena. She wants to know if I want to go out tonight. I wonder if I shouldn't just stay home. But why should I? I'm tired of being alone.

I send her a text and ask where we're going.

I open the door to the bar; I can't see Jimena anywhere. Maybe she's in the bathroom or maybe she's running late.

I sit down by the counter and order vodka with diet coke.

I take a sip of my drink. The vodka is cheap; it tastes more like cleaning solvent. But then again, it's cheap and that's all I care about.

I feel someone watching me. I glance to my right. A man

dressed in a blue shirt and jeans is staring at me from the other end of the bar. I look away. I hope Jimena will show up before the man decides to try to talk to me. I never know how to tell people I'm not interested. Besides, American men seem to have a hard time understanding the word "no." They're nothing like Finnish men; men in Finland know how to accept defeat without an argument. I never realized how kind that is until I came here.

I see Jimena half-running across the room. She stops in front of me and takes a deep breath.

"*¡Lo siento, cariño!* Bus bunching."

She takes off her heavy winter coat and sits down next to me. Her hair is gathered in a loose bun and she is wearing a lipstick that matches her tight red pullover. She looks as if she just stepped out of a salon. I know I look like a mouse compared to her, but I don't mind. It means people won't notice me and that's a good thing. Jimena smiles and orders a cocktail. I sip my drink and wait for her to tell me the reason for her good mood.

"*¡Ay,* Marja! I'm so happy! We *finally* got all the paperwork filed this morning! Now we just have to wait for the embassy to process them."

I congratulate Jimena and try to smile, but the smile doesn't materialize. I'm glad for her, of course I am. It's just hard to share in someone else's joy when my own life seems to be just an endless series of disasters.

"He's gone, huh?"

"Yeah," I say, staring at my glass.

"How did he take it?"

"I don't know. Not well?"

"That's his problem. The best thing is to move on as quickly as possible. Do you still have the Tinder app?"

"I do, but I don't think—"

"Oh, come on! It'll be fun!"

"But they're all just looking for sex," I say with a groan.

"Well, that's the point!" says Jimena laughing. "Give me your phone, I'll help you look."

I hand my phone over to Jimena reluctantly. She swipes to the left a couple of times. She stops and looks at a picture.

"Aww… he looks cute, yes?"

I glance at the photo. I agree he's cute, but he's far too young. He looks as if he's barely out of high school. I tell Jimena as much.

"The young ones are the fun ones!" laughs Jimena.

I try not to sigh. I know Greg is gone and that he'll never come back, but the idea of being with someone else at this point feels like adultery. Technically it is, but maybe Jimena is right. Maybe it doesn't matter. Greg cheated on me plenty and he's on Tinder too. I assume he's not there only to admire profile pictures.

"*Ay,* I like this one!"

I look at the picture and shrug.

"He looks okay."

"Just okay? ¡*Ay,* Marja! You need to loosen up a little! Let's like his profile, that way you two can message each other."

Jimena's eyes light up.

"He liked you too! *Perfecto!* Let's send him a message!"

I look at Jimena, my eyes filled with horror. I try to tell her that it's a *really* bad idea, but it's too late. She has already typed a message and sent it.

"What did you write?" I ask, holding my breath.

"That you want to make his night," says Jimena with a smile that leaves nothing for the imagination. I close my eyes. I would never have said such a thing. I hope he doesn't answer.

"Oh! He wants to know when you're available to meet. What should we say? I know! Let's invite him over here!"

"No, don't!" I say and look at Jimena with pleading eyes. She puts her hand on my arm and gives me look; it's the look she gives me every time she thinks I'm not thinking straight.

"*Listen!* You need to do this! You need to get that ex-husband out of your head!"

"He's not my ex-husband yet," I say with a far more sullen voice than I intended to.

"He will be soon *and* he'll be *so* jealous!"

I look at Jimena and wonder why I would want to make Greg jealous. I don't want to have anything to do with him. I don't even want to think about him.

Jimena sends another message and puts my phone on the counter.

"And now we wait," she says with a sly smile.

I try to smile. I know Jimena means well, but sometimes she is beyond overbearing without even realizing it.

"Aww… Carlos sent a picture from a party!"

I watch as Jimena types. Her husband must have said something funny, because she giggles. I know Jimena will be occupied talking to her husband at least a half an hour. I order another drink and turn to stare at the TV screen.

I can feel cold air enter the room.

I glance at the front door.

I nearly drop my glass.

It's my Tinder date.

11

I look at my phone. It's almost eleven. I get up and go to the bathroom. I look at myself in the mirror. A large smile appears on my face.

I did it!

I wonder for a moment why I feel such a sense of victory over a one-night-stand. It doesn't make any sense although at the same time it makes all the sense in the world. I told Greg to fuck off in the only way possible. I said it with my body.

Jimena was right. I feel better now.

I go to the living room and find a scarf on the couch. I bury my face in it. I can smell his scent on it.

Tom.

My Tinder date.

He wasn't bad in bed, but he wasn't great either. I'm sure I wasn't all that great either. The first time is usually like trying to sing a duet without ever having practiced together. The harmony isn't there. It's more like two people doing their own thing, hoping the other will catch up.

There will be no second date. I told Tom I wasn't looking for anything long term. He said he understood and left before sunrise. I'm grateful he did; that way neighbors won't ask any questions. I laugh at the thought for a moment. It's not as if they have ever shown any interest.

They are the good kind; the kind that don't poke their

noses into everyone else's business.

My cat follows me to the kitchen. I watch as it eats the colorful fish-shaped pebbles with focused concentration. I lean against the counter and wait for my coffee to brew. I try to come up with something to do that doesn't cost any money. It's my day off and I want to do something other than spend the whole day on the couch like I usually do. Maybe I should go for a walk by the lake. The longer I think about it, the better the idea sounds.

I close the gate and walk to Division Street.

I don't have to wait long until the bus arrives. I take a seat in the middle and pretend to look at my phone to avoid the eyes that stare at me from the other side of the aisle. I've never understood why some people think staring is okay. In my opinion it's ill-mannered to make people feel self-conscious. But then again, I don't think most Americans even know what that feels like.

We're almost in the city when three teenaged girls get on the bus. They remain standing next to me although there are plenty of empty seats. They giggle and laugh. I try to tune them out, but their high-pitched voices fill the bus.

"No, it happened in Philadelphia! The guy was running toward the train and tried to get on and then he got hit by the train!" says the girl with a long ponytail and braces.

The other two girls roll their eyes and laugh.

I want to roll my eyes too. I've noticed stupidity is a

favorite subject among teens here. They have an obsessive need to affirm that at least they aren't *that* stupid. The stifling fear of making a mistake was hammered in them as children and it never leaves them alone although they are filled with confidence in every other way.

It's just another oddity here.

I get off the bus and walk to the beach. It's cold although the sun is shining. I look at the lake that glimmers under the bright winter sun. It's as if the sky and the lake have merged into a glittering mass of moving molecules. It's hard to tell where the horizon begins and ends.

I walk along the shore and think about my life. I'm going home in a few months, but there's nothing waiting for me there. I know I still have my family and friends, I haven't been gone that long, but what am I going to do? I have a High School diploma, but it doesn't get me very far. I could try to get into the university again, but I'm not so sure it's going to work any better this time. I suppose I could go traveling like some do, but that requires money and to get money I need to get a job and none of the jobs I can get pay well enough. It's an endless cycle of maybes that never become a yes.

I watch as the wind whips the water. It reminds me of our wedding day. The downpour began at the worst possible moment, followed by thunder and lighting. I sat in the car and watched as the sky flashed white every few seconds. I was afraid I was going to ruin my dress if I got out. Not that I had to walk very far; just a few steps from the car to the midsized suburban ranch house owned by Greg's aunt. We had the ceremony in her living room. Greg didn't know how to plan a wedding, I couldn't do it from Finland, and the idea of going to City Hall didn't appeal to either of us. We didn't have too many people to invite anyway and it kept the budget to a minimum. Saving money was more important than having a lavish wedding. It's at least what Greg said. He said he didn't have any money. It was just another lie. At least that particular lie had a silver lining to it. I'm glad we didn't spend too much on our wedding since our marriage didn't last that long. I've heard enough stories of people who continue to pay for the wedding long after the marriage has already ended. It's just adding insult to the injury, a constant reminder of what could have been, but never was.

I pick up a stone from the sand. It's shaped like a heart. Everywhere I go I'm reminded of love. It's as if the whole universe taunts me and wants to remind me how I've failed. But I didn't fail. I *did* love Greg. He just didn't know how to love me back.

I think of Tom for a moment. I try to imagine what it would be like to be his girlfriend, but the image is like a hologram that flickers and never stabilizes. I feel just as much toward him as I feel toward the stone I'm holding in my hand. It's strange how sex bonds sometimes, but other times, even when you want it to, it doesn't. In one way I'm grateful. The last thing I need right now is another broken heart before my heart has even had a chance to heal.

I turn around and begin to walk back. The wind blows my

hood off. I leave it be; my hat will keep me warm. I watch as the sun vanishes behind a cloud. The water turns dark as if the lake has swallowed the glimmering light in one big gulp.

I glance at the heart-shaped stone in my hand. I throw it into the lake.

I notice my wedding ring.

I pull it off my finger and throw it as far as I can.

Goodbye marriage.

You belong in the lake too.

12

I look around the living room. Greg came by yesterday and took most things. I don't have a TV anymore, and the kitchen table is gone too. He left the couch, because I was sitting on it and he didn't want to argue with me in front of his friend. He left the cat too. He didn't even look at it.

"I guess he didn't care about either of us," I say and pet my cat. It purrs and closes its eyes. I wonder if it knows what I'm talking about.

"I need to go to the store. Do you want to come with me?"

My cat gives me an annoyed look.

"*Et tietenkään.* Of course you don't want to come. It's cold outside."

I get up and go to the bedroom. I need to bundle up or I'll turn into an icicle before I've even reached the bus stop.

I lock the door to my apartment. The cold wind hits my face the moment I step outside. I feel my whole body chill instantly. Nordic winters aren't kind, but the Midwestern cold digs into your bones and makes you feel you're freezing from within. Not to mention what the dry air does to your skin and hair. I wish I could fill the bathtub with moisturizer and soak in it for an hour. How anyone deals with winters in Chicago is a mystery to me. Only a seal has the ability to endure this kind of weather. I adjust my scarf until only my eyes are visible. I know I look like an old woman who has seen better days. I don't care. Staying warm is more important than making a fashion statement.

The bus arrives mercifully on time. I take a seat in the middle and pretend I don't notice anyone. I get off two stops later and cross North Avenue.

The bus arrives a few minutes later. I get on and walk to the back. I lean against the barrier that separates the back door from the back of the bus. The bus isn't too crowded, but I prefer to stand on this route. It's only four stops, but there is always someone who tells me I have a pretty smile and tries to get my phone number. As long as I stand by the door I'm left alone; exiting people don't have the time to stop to have a conversation.

I watch as a young woman pushes a stroller into the bus. She is carrying a backpack with neon pink straps and she looks like any other teenager on her way to school, except her eyes behind the smart glasses reflect anxiety and the baby in the stroller can't be older than a few months. I feel sorry for her. I'm sure she didn't expect her life to turn out the way it did. I want to tell her everything will turn out all right, but I can't tell her that. I don't even know if my own life will turn out all right.

I get off the bus at Kostner Avenue and begin to walk toward Aldi. I look at the deserted streets. Everyone is hiding in their homes. I wish I was home too, but I have no choice. Being hungry is worse than being cold.

The moment I reach the carts outside the store I remember the quarter that is sitting on the kitchen counter. No quarter means no cart and that means I can only buy the items I can carry with my hands. And *that* means I'll have to come back in a couple of days.

I let out a frustrated sigh.

I see an old man exiting the store. He must have seen my frustration because he leaves his cart right in front of me and walks away. I call after him and tell him I don't have a quarter to give him.

He just waves and smiles.

The sudden act of kindness brings tears to my eyes. Or maybe it's the cold weather.

I tell myself it's the weather.

Crying is a sign of weakness and I'm not weak. I'm stupid and gullible, but not weak. Or maybe I'm weak too and crying has nothing to do with weakness. Maybe it takes strength to cry. I tell myself to think about it later. It's too cold to stand outside wondering about all the reasons people cry.

I enter the store and push my cart along the wide aisles. I look at the colorful packages. Mexican corn chips blend effortlessly with German chocolates and Italian wines. Aldi is as international as the world itself. It's comforting in a way.

I pick two bottles of wine from the shelf. I know I need to drink less, but that is going to have to wait. I can't face these endless months without the help of wine. It was how I got through my days with Greg too, especially in the end. I waited till I couldn't wait any longer, then I drank.

I push my cart to the checkout line. I smile at the cashier who slides my items quickly over the scanner into another cart. I wonder if she was born here or if she came here. Her English is flawless and her movements have the confident briskness only Americans seem to possess. But she has also a relaxed smile combined with a curious hardness in her eyes; a subtle kind of stoicism. I conclude she was born here, but to immigrant parents.

I don't even know why I'm wondering about such things. I guess being here has changed me. I've noticed Americans want to know everything about the person they meet. In Finland everyone minds their own business and says a brief hello if absolutely necessary. My neighbors wouldn't even leave their apartments if they heard someone was in the stairwell. But perhaps at some level curiosity is to be expected. Culture isn't something that can be hidden or erased completely. It's like a faded stamp that is hard to see, but is there nevertheless. I just wish people would realize wondering where someone is from and asking about it are two different things. It would make me feel more included. I already know it's a wish that will never come true. Everything around me is designed to constantly remind me I'm an immigrant, a legal alien.

I don't belong.

13

I get on the bus and press my card against the reader.

I feel like a wet mop. The closer we get to Christmas the crazier work gets. I look for a seat. I have no luck this time; the bus is jam-packed. I hold on to the metal pole and try to steady myself. I don't want to be thrown against the other passengers. Not that there is much risk of it. It's as if we're human sardines lined up in a moving metal tin.

The bus slows down and stops several times before we have even reached the next stop. I look up and down the street through the window. The traffic isn't moving in either direction. If I stay on this bus, it'll be midnight until I get home.

I get off the bus at State Street and take the stairs down to the Red Line. I stand by a pillar and watch as tourists take selfies against the holiday train on the opposite platform. They laugh and look surprised as if the train has arrived from another planet just to amuse them. It's strange how an ordinary train becomes the object of curiosity just because someone tossed a bit of garland and color on it. Most Chicagoans hardly notice the train even as the step into it.

"Excuse me, Miss?"

I turn my head and see a man whose face is as dark as the Nordic night in December.

"Does this train go to Montrose?"

"I… don't know. There's a… a…...map… on the wall."

I point to the wall and feel my cheeks flush. When you think in Finnish, the words don't want to come out in English. He probably thinks I'm not all there.

The man smiles and thanks me. I'm about to turn around when something about his eyes makes me look at him again. His eyes are kind and they shine like stars. They don't have the same strange glaze I see in most people's eyes here; the lackluster dimness that resembles pea soup. He must be a visitor. Or maybe he lives here and everyone thinks he's just a tourist. It shouldn't matter, but it does.

I hear a whooshing sound and turn to look instinctively to my left. A bright light appears in the tunnel. I turn to look at the man again, but he has already disappeared. I feel oddly disappointed. Something about him made me feel at home. As if he wasn't pretending to be someone he wasn't like most people here.

I wait for the train to come to a halt. I can smell the booze the moment I enter the train. A young man wearing an ugly Christmas sweater asks people if they have holiday cheer. His friend, who is wearing an ill-fitting red suit, chimes in. When people don't answer, they tell them they are getting coal for Christmas. I want to stop them and tell them Santa Claus doesn't hand out coal. He lives in Rovaniemi as every Finn knows and there are no coal mines nearby. I want to tell them the Santa they love so much wouldn't exist if it wasn't for immigrants; that Santa was designed by the son of a Finnish immigrant. I want to tell them immigrants matter, that they should be kinder to us. But I know they wouldn't listen.

I look out the window and try to ignore the young men as much as I can, but there is no ignoring the terrible bellowing of Jingle Bells that fills the whole train car. I block my ears and stare at the dark wall outside the doors hoping they would just stop. It's not the first time I find myself missing the stoic public silence you find everywhere in Finland. Why people feel they have the right to impose themselves on everyone else in public is just beyond me.

The train arrives at Clark. I get off as quickly as possible. I see a dozen drunken young men pour out of the train. They seem to have a splendid time the way drunken people always do before they become either sleepy or quarrelsome. I want to avoid getting stuck in the middle of them. I half-run to the escalator and manage to get on it before the rowdy group begins to move.

I resurface at street level and look around. The traffic isn't moving here either. The city streets seem to have transformed into a massive parking lot for some reason. It makes no sense—unless there's an event going on somewhere and they've blocked off some of the streets. They do it here regularly as if people don't have anywhere they need to be.

I stare at Clark Street hoping to see the bus.

Ten agonizing minutes later I see the bus making its way slowly through the traffic. The driver manages to turn to Division Street after yet another five minutes of waiting.
The crowd that has been waiting for the bus has grown by the minute. Luckily the bus is nearly empty; we'll all fit in.

I take a seat in the middle of the bus. A young man and a couple sit down on the opposite side. I glance at them a few times and wonder why the couple looks so uncomfortable. The young man leans forward the way people do when they are sitting in a waiting room. The young woman next to him leans back, clearly wishing she wasn't in the bus. Something about the young woman makes me look at her again. She's wearing no makeup other than deep red lipstick. It's almost as if she has crushed a handful of cherries and applied the juice to her lips. Her youthful lips hold the color well; there are no wrinkles for the color to bleed into.

A few stops later the young men get up and leave the bus; the young woman remains behind. I realize they weren't a couple after all. It explains the young man's tense posture and the young woman's cold demeanor. He wanted her attention and she rejected him. The scene reminds me that I liked a few profiles on the Tinder app last night out of sheer boredom. I'm sure all of them have ignored me. To prove myself right, I pull my phone from my pocket and open the app. To my great surprise I notice I have three new messages.

I click on the first message.

"Would you ever want to have a little freedom in a relationship that was more long term?"

No, ei! I don't think so!

Next.

"I'd walk all the way to Chicago just for one kiss."

I bet you would.

"Hi, I'm Jake and I just moved back to Chicago from California. Why did I leave just before the winter? Anyways I'm tall, athletic and very sarcastic and still adapting to the cold."

Hmm... ehkä, maybe.

I look again at his pictures.

Definitely!

He looks like someone fun to hang out with for a few days. I stare out the window and bite my lower lip. What do people say to make themselves sound interesting? I wish Jimena was sitting next to me right now. She'd know what to say. The idea pops suddenly in my head. I'm going to tell him I would love to keep him warm. Jimena would approve of it.

I type the message and hit send.

I regret it instantaneously.

I stare at my phone. I'm beginning to think I should delete the whole app and be done with it. The thought brings Jimena's face before my eyes, halfway berating me, halfway encouraging me. Her eyes tell me I need to live a little and not be so afraid. I know she's right. I need to learn to relax. I don't even know why I feel so insecure. I mean, I know why, but I'm in America now. No one likes a grey mouse or a brown mouse here. No one likes mice, period. This is my chance to become something different, a more confident version of myself. I have to take it.

My phone beeps.

It's Jake.

He's wondering if I'm free tomorrow.

14

I look around the crowded room.

There is no sign of Jake. I tell myself to stop being ridiculous. I know I'm early. He'll probably show up soon. Or maybe he won't. Maybe he took another look at my picture and decided to ghost me, maybe—

I take a deep breath.

Rauhoitu. Just relax.

I stand by the entrance and watch as people stand in groups as if to protect themselves from other people. The younger they are, the closer they stand to each other. I've never understood why people go out only to hang out with their friends. Isn't meeting new people the whole point? But maybe it isn't here. I don't know how Americans do most things. It's all confusing.

"Maria?"

I turn around and see Jake standing a few steps from me. He's wearing light blue jeans and a black sweater underneath his winter coat.

"Oh, hi," I say and try my hardest not to blush.

Jake gives me a side hug; the kind that leaves maximum amount of space between our bodies.

"Should we get something to drink?"

"Yeah, sure."

I follow him to the bar. I order vodka. I need to quiet my

nerves or I might just run away. There's something about Jake that makes me nervous. Or maybe it's me. Maybe I'm making myself nervous.

"You have an accent, where are you from?"

I try not to look annoyed. If I got a dollar every time someone asks that question at work I would be able to buy a ticket back home in no time.

"Finland."

"Finland, huh? So, what brought you here?"

"The old story, I got married."

"Oh?" says Jake, frowning slightly.

"I mean, it's over. We're just waiting for the paperwork, you know, the divorce papers," I say quickly, blushing.

"Aww… that's rough. I'm sorry."

"It's okay. So, where are you from? I mean, not you. Your grandparents, or your parents—" I say stumbling over my words. I finish my drink in one quick sweep. I need to seriously calm down.

"I got you. My mom is from Jamaica and my dad is from Spain."

"How did they meet?"

"The other old story, they came here to study and stayed."

"Have you ever been to Spain?"

"No. But I want to go."

"You should! It's nice. I went there a few years ago with my best friend Sara."

"So you're a world traveler," says Jake, smiling.

"Not exactly," I say laughing. "For us going to Spain is

like you going to Mexico."

"Ah, that makes sense. Do you want another drink?" asks Jake, pointing at my empty glass.

"Sure."

"What do you want?"

"Surprise me," I say, trying to sound lighthearted.

Jake orders shots of tequila. I look at the shot glasses and swallow hard. Tequila and I haven't been friends since I drank too much of it on my twenty-first birthday and woke up the next day feeling as if a truck had driven over my head. Jake raises a glass and waits for me to grab one. I pick up one of the shot glasses and stare at the golden liquid for a few seconds. I down it in one quick sweep. I shake my head as the alcohol makes my body contract as if it has received a shock.

Three shots later the room begins to spin all around me. I tell Jake I'll be right back and get up. I join the line of giggling women who are waiting outside of the bathroom. I shake my head to get my brain working again. It's not smart to get drunk on a date, especially not on a first date. I cover my mouth quickly to suffocate the laughter that wants out. I just realized I'm on a date with a man I met on Tinder while I'm married to a man who fucks his ex-wife. No one is ever going to believe me back home. I wouldn't. It's like I'm a star in a soap opera—my very own soap opera.

I make my way back to the bar through the crowd. I can see Jake talking to a woman.

For a moment everything stops moving around me.

I reach the bar and look at Jake with apprehension. He

smiles at me.

The woman turns around.

"Marja! You're here!" exclaims Jimena and gives me a hug. She looks at Jake, then back at me. Her lips form into a knowing smile.

In a moment's flash it all becomes clear.

This is a set up.

Jimena must have told Jake to take me out on a date. It's the only reason he wanted to go out with me in the first place. She's probably been here this whole time, watching us. The humiliation makes my face burn.

I grab my jacket from the chair and walk quickly to the front door.

"Marja, where are you going?" calls Jimena after me.

She runs after me and grabs my arm.

"Hey, where are you going?"

"Home," I say coldly.

"*¿Por que?* Why?"

"I don't need your help! I don't even want to date! I'm still married! I did it just to make you happy and then you have to… *do this*!"

"What are you talking about?"

"You told Jake to take me out!"

"No I didn't."

"Then why are you here?"

"I'm here for my cousin's birthday."

"Is Jake your cousin?"

"No, but he knows my brother Pablo. They've been friends forever. I was just saying hi. I haven't seen him for a while, not since he moved to California."

I stare at Jimena. The feeling of humiliation begins to give way to the realization she is telling the truth. I waver for a moment, but then I tell myself I don't care anymore.

"Tell Jake I went home," I say and open the front door.

"Marja, wait! Come back!"

I exit the bar and begin to walk toward the bus stop.

My very own soap opera.

It got a fitting end, that's all I can say.

15

I close the gate and walk quickly to the bus stop.

I look up toward the sky. I can smell snow in the air. I hope the snow won't show up for at least a few more days. I really need new winter shoes, but I can't afford them, just as I can't afford most of the basic things I need to live. I'm reminded of all the stories my grandparents told me when I was growing up, about the poverty and misery they experienced when they were young. I never thought the richest country in the world would have the same problems tiny poverty-stricken Finland had after Winter War.

The bus arrives. I press my card against the reader and walk to the back.

"Come on, you with the red jacket! I'm talking to you. Come up here!" says the driver, looking at the rearview mirror.

I look around. I see a heavy-set man two rows behind me. He gives the driver a defiant look.

"Come on, man! Come up here!"

The man gets up finally and moves slowly to the front.

"I told you, you gotta pay your fare!" says the driver, emphasizing the last words.

The man mumbles something.

"No, no, you got to pay now! I'm trying to be courteous here."

The man mumbles something again.

"No! *You* got to get the change! There's another bus coming after this one."

A young man gets up and pays the man's fare. The man with the red jacket turns around and tells the driver to shut up as he walks back to the end of the bus. I look at the man as he passes me. He isn't the first one who's tried to get a free ride. I find it odd how some people expect to get away with it. But I guess I shouldn't be surprised about anything anymore.

I notice a young woman on the other side of the aisle. She's eating fried chicken from a box tucked in a plastic bag with a large yellow smiley face on it. She has a careful look about her, the almost apologizing appearance of a person who knows she shouldn't be eating in the bus, but who has decided she wants to eat the chicken while it's still warm. She finishes the piece in her hand, closes the bag carefully, and settles into staring out of the window for the rest of the ride. Maybe she noticed that I glanced at her a few times.

A moment later a woman answers her phone. I try not to listen, but her voice fills the entire bus.

"No, no kissing until payday. No, I said no kissing until payday!"

I turn my head slightly and glance at the woman. She looks middle-aged but she could be younger. It's hard to tell. Stress and worry could have left its mark on her face instead of age. I listen to her go on about how she needs the money first before kissing. I cringe a little. She makes it sound too much like prostitution. But then again, if the options are poverty or enough money to eat, why shouldn't she require the money before the kisses? Clearly she has learned something from her past mistakes. I can only think how I need to do the same. I can't afford any more of these clusterfucks that leave me hanging in the wind like a dead leaf every single time. I have to begin to build my life instead of tearing it apart every time I get a great idea that leads nowhere.

I get off the bus and walk slowly down Michigan Avenue. I try to think of what I should say to Jimena. She tried to call me yesterday. Jake tried to call me too. I feel embarrassed and annoyed. Embarrassed because I know I acted like a child. Annoyed because Jimena assumes everyone will react the way she does in every situation. Just because she knows how to brush off everything doesn't mean I do. I don't have the confidence everyone else has in this country. I wish I did, it would make my life so much easier.

But I don't and I probably never will.

I know I'm supposed to apologize, but I don't want to. I'm tired of apologizing for situations other people have created that have nothing to do with me. How was I supposed to know Jimena's brother knew Jake? I'm sure most people would have reacted the same way I did. Or maybe I'm just overreacting. Greg always said I did.

I enter the mall and find my way to the store. I'm almost

at the service counter when Jimena taps my left shoulder and hugs me as I turn around.

"*Lo siento, cariño.* I know why you got angry. I would have done the same thing if I were you."

"It's okay," I say, and look away.

"No, it's not okay! Jake was sad that you left. He said he really liked you."

I look at Jimena. I wonder if she's just trying to cheer me up like she always does or if she's telling the truth. I've never heard her lie, so assume she's doing a bit of both. I'm relieved I don't have to try to explain or apologize. Jimena is my only friend here and losing a friend who has done nothing but be nice to me would hurt more than losing a husband who did little other than hurt me.

The manager stops next to me and tells me she needs me to do folding duty; a few tables need to be straightened up. I nod and walk to one of the displays next to the register. I stare at the jumbled mess. I don't see the point. The clothes are going to be all over the table in less than an hour. It's like shoveling while it's still snowing.

A man stops to look at the sweaters on the other side of the display. I can feel him looking at me. I want to ask him to stop staring at me, but I know I can't. I'm on display too.

"Do you like this color?"

I look up.

"It's okay," I say with an awkward smile.

"What size do you wear? I'll buy it for you."

"Oh… no…. If they see you buying it for me, I'll get fired."

"Well, we can't have that. How about if I buy it for you and you can meet me outside the store in a few minutes?"

"I can't leave the store."

"Wow, they make this really difficult. Okay, well, I'll tell you what, I will leave the bag at the concierge desk downstairs. You can pick it up from there. What's your name?"

"Mar—Maria."

"Okay, Maria. Is this the right size for you?"

I look at the tag.

"Yes."

I watch as the man walks over to the service counter and pays for the sweater. He waves at me as he leaves the store.

Shit!

I'm going to get in trouble for this.

I walk quickly to the register and pull Jimena over to the side.

"Someone just bought a sweater for me and said he was going to leave it downstairs. What should I do?"

"Pick it up," says Jimena shrugging.

"But won't I get in trouble?"

"Why? The company made money."

I bite my lower lip.

"But won't he expect me to give him something?"

"That's his problem. You're not a *prostituta*."

"So, I should pick it up?"

"If you don't, someone else will."

I look away for a moment.

"Did you like it? The sweater?" asks Jimena.

"I did, it's one of the new ones."

"Then pick it up!"

"Okay!"

I return to the display and glance around. I try to make myself as inconspicuous as possible.

Hopefully no one else is going to try to buy me something.

16

I put on the sweater Robert bought me. He left me his phone number in the bag. I texted him to say thank you. I knew it was a mistake when he asked if I wanted to go out. I told him I was married; he responded with a smiley face— then nothing. I'm beginning to think I shouldn't have gotten rid of my wedding ring. I've noticed the assumption here is that no ring means you're available.

I go to the bathroom and look at myself in the mirror. The deep red color suits me. I'm glad Robert bought the sweater for me although he was a bit of a sleazoid. I wouldn't have had anything nice to wear today if he hadn't. I arrived with only one suitcase and most of my clothes have reached their expiration date. Looking nice at Christmas is still important to me, especially since Jimena invited me to celebrate Christmas with her family.

I tried to tell her I couldn't possibly intrude, but she just shook her head to tell me to stop being silly. "You can't be alone on Christmas, it's not right," she said with the tone she always uses when she disapproves of something. I did decline attending Mass the next morning though. Jimena just laughed and told me God would forgive me, but only because I was a white as snow. I didn't know what she meant by it and I didn't ask. Maybe it had something to do with Jimena's conviction we're all innocent and sin is just a human invention to make us feel guilty for having normal human feelings.

I'm not getting any presents this year but I don't care. I'm just glad to spend the day with someone other than my cat. I did promise my cat I would bring it a treat. Even cats deserve to be happy on Christmas.

I finish my makeup and smile at my own image. I look nice, even though I'm the one saying it. I look at my hair for a second. I suppose I should bleach my hair again to hide the growth, but I like my natural hair color; it's the color of wet straw when it has dried under the hot summer sun. Greg insisted I should bleach it; he said it made me look sexy. I didn't want to, but I did it to please him. Maybe I don't need to keep on doing it now that he's gone.

I stare at myself for a moment. My eyes are light gray, the same shade as a grey wolf's fur. My lips are what you would call average; they aren't bee-stung or too thin. My nose is straight and my eyebrows make me look serious. I'm so average it hurts. I have no idea why anyone would find me attractive; so few Finnish men ever did. I know what Jimena said, but it's still mystifying. But why am I even thinking about it now?

I know why.

Jimena hinted there would be someone at the party I might be interested in. She hasn't stopped trying to set me up even after I told her I was done with dating. I deleted the Tinder app to make sure I wouldn't try to find another date in the middle of the night when sleep eludes me.

I go to the living room. I put on my shoes and hope the

mystery person is a visiting relative who speaks Spanish and I have to only smile the night away.

I can only be so lucky.

The bus arrives.

I find a seat in the middle of the bus. I notice a young woman on the other side of the aisle. She sits by the aisle as if she wishes to prevent anyone from sitting next to her. It's clear she's not used to taking the bus. The way she sits absolutely still and clutches her bag with her hands tells me all about it.

I look away, but after a moment my eyes find her again. Something about her profile makes me think of old portraits of Victorian women. Her gaze is lowered and her straight brown hair falls to her shoulders from underneath her stiff felt hat. Her jacket is made out of stiff grey wool and her knee-length high heel boots look unforgivingly tight.

I watch as she takes a small coin purse from her stiff leather bag. She begins to move coins from one pocket to the other. Maybe she is counting them or maybe she likes to have certain coins in certain pockets. I can't tell. Suddenly she turns her head and I see her eyes. She is much younger than I expected; younger and insecure. It explains the inward pointing toes and her stiff demeanor. She isn't comfortable with her own appearance. She is like a doll that someone else has dressed.

A man sits down next to me. I turn to look out the

window.

I feel annoyed.

People always get in the way of people watching.

I get off the bus and walk down the street. After a few minutes I find the right house. I text Jimena to let her know I'm outside. She rushes down the stairs and opens the gate for me. She wishes me Merry Christmas in Spanish and kisses me on both cheeks. Somehow she manages to do so without smearing her lipstick all over my cheeks.

I look at Jimena. She's wearing a tight red dress and large silver hoops. She looks as if she just came from a modeling job. I try not to be jealous, but it's impossible not to be. I know I'm not the only one who has felt the twinge of jealousy standing next to her, but at the same time I can't think of another person who has been kinder to me than Jimena. She doesn't ever put me down. Instead she's always trying to make me feel better about myself. I know I'm beyond lucky to have her as my friend.

I walk up the steps after Jimena and enter an apartment. I smile at a woman who says *Feliz Navidad* as she passes me. I look around for a moment unsure where to go. Jimena puts her hands on my shoulders and turns me to the right.

"Miguel, this is Marja; Marja, meet Miguel."

"*Hola,* Marja. *Feliz Navidad*, Merry Christmas."

I begin to say hello, but the word gets stuck somewhere. I'm looking straight into the softest brown eyes I've ever seen. I feel as if I'm staring at Jimena, but the expression doesn't match. Jimena looks at the world through playful, teasing eyes. Miguel's eyes are playful, but there is an endless depth to them as if pools of water hide behind them. I feel as if I'm drowning and being rescued at the same time. I look at him, unable to move.

Miguel moves closer and hugs me. He smells as if he has just come from an orchard where ripe fruit and clean air mingle together creating a scent of freshness. I don't know if he's wearing cologne or if it's his natural scent. It doesn't matter. I want to stay in his arms forever.

No! I'm not doing this again!

I pull myself away abruptly. I spot the bathroom with my left eye. I mumble something about needing to use it.

I slip into the small room that has more beauty products on the shelves than I've owned my entire life. I sit down on the toilet seat and try to steady my breathing. Why do I do this to myself every time? Why do I lose my ability to think every time I come near a good-looking man? I wouldn't be here if I knew how to use my head once in a while.

I stare at the wall. I know I can't stay here forever, but I'm not sure how I'm going to be in the same room with Miguel without losing myself in his eyes. It always begins that way and then it ends. I'm beginning to feel depressed when the thought comes to me like an approaching bright light on a dark winter road. It's the realization I'm still married.

That's all I need to say.

I get up and look at myself in the mirror to make sure my lipstick hasn't smeared. I stare at my own reflection for a moment and close my eyes briefly. I feel like an idiot. Why did I think Miguel would be interested in me? I know he was just being nice to me because I'm Jimena's friend. I'm sure he's wondering why I was acting so weird. I need to get my act together.

I straighten my sweater and take a deep breath.

Ei mitään hätää; nothing to worry about.

I can do this.

I leave the bathroom and walk into the living room. Jimena appears from nowhere and grabs my arm. She pulls me to a table covered in foil containers, tells me the names of all the dishes and gives me a plate. I look at all the food. I feel as if I've died and gone to heaven.

Free food and lots of it!

It's not like Christmas food at home, but I don't care. I pile rice and lamb on my plate until I can't see the paper plate anymore. I take a seat in a corner and look at the food in front of me. It's the true Christmas miracle, the one everyone should be singing about. Who cares about peace on earth; people need to eat. That's what's important.

I take a bite and close my eyes. Even the taste is heavenly. I realize it's not the food that is making me happy. It's the fact that someone cooked it for me. I know they didn't think of me, but I was invited to eat, so they cooked it for me. Jimena was right, humans aren't meant to be alone on Christmas, and they certainly aren't meant to eat frozen pizza most days of the week. They are meant to be with people and eat food—real food.

Jimena sits down next to me and puts a beer bottle in front of me. She smiles and begins to teach me Spanish words out of the blue. I suspect she's had a bit to drink already. She applauds and cheers when she realizes I know how to pronounce the words right because I can roll my r's. I'm beginning to wonder why she's so enthusiastic. A moment later it dawns on me. She's trying to get me together with Miguel, although I don't know what knowing a few Spanish words would do. Miguel speaks perfect English, much better than I do.

Jimena glances at Miguel and smiles at me.

"*So*... what do you think? He's a catch, no?"

I see Miguel smiling at me from the other side of the room. I try to smile, but the smile dies before it ever reaches my lips.

I don't need this!

What am I saying? This is exactly what I need. I need someone who is kind; someone who isn't a self-absorbed narcissist who runs back to his ex-wife every time she calls.

I saw them together yesterday. I had to duck behind the register to avoid being seen. They were out buying last minute Christmas presents, walking hand-in-hand as if she had never divorced him and he had never married me. I'm beginning to think Alene plays a cat and mouse game with Greg too. All I can think is that they deserve each other.

I glance at Miguel. He is talking to someone I think is Jimena's brother. I'm still not sure what relation Miguel is to Jimena, but I think they are cousins. Everyone else seems to be siblings, uncles and aunts, but I don't know who belongs to whom.

I turn to tell Jimena that I agree with her, but she has

already vanished. I look at the beer bottle on the table. I know I shouldn't drink it, but I feel suddenly sorry for myself. Sorry for everything that has happened and all the things that will never happen and the mess my life has become.

I down the whole bottle in one sweep. As soon as I have finished it, I see Jimena appear from the kitchen. She brings me another beer, then a shot of tequila, then another.

I drink as if there is no tomorrow.

I don't want there to be another tomorrow.

I want this misery to end already. Waiting for months for a freedom I should never have lost is a cruel punishment. Being married to a man like Greg is even more so.

I drink until my head feels wobbly as if all brain cells have gelled with the alcohol. I shouldn't have had the last shot or the one before that. I try to get up, but my legs refuse to work. I can feel someone leading me across the living room. After a few steps I feel a soft bed underneath me. I try to see the person's face, but all I can see is a dark figure against the light.

I close my eyes and smile.

At least I won't be alone tonight.

17

I wake up.

My mouth feels metallic and dry. Something inside my head keeps on pounding as if it wants to come out.

I lean my weight against my left elbow. I'm about to throw the blanket off when I suddenly stop. I see stuffed animals on the shelf. I glance at the blanket: it's covered in fire trucks, dogs, and cartoon people.

Why am I sleeping in a child's room?

Slowly the previous night comes back to me. I cover my eyes with my right hand and lay back down for a moment.

Voi ei! Oh no!

I made a total fool out of myself. I'll never be able to look Jimena in the eyes again.

I get up and walk slowly to the door. I peek into the hallway. It's empty. Everyone must have gone to the Christmas Mass. I sneak into the bathroom and brush my teeth with my right index finger. I find a hairbrush and brush my hair quickly. I look at myself in the mirror. My makeup is smeared. I'm going to have to wash it off or I'll look like I've slept somewhere other than my own bed, which is true, but the assumption will be that I didn't sleep alone. I don't need that kind of judgment today.

I look at the shelf. I find a bottle that looks like makeup remover. I scrub my face and look at myself in the mirror again. I'm as pale as a bleached sheet.

Just another not-so-great Christmas in this country.

I glance at the clock on the wall above the toilet. It's just past seven. I don't know when the Mass ends. Everyone might be coming back soon. I need to get out of here.

I walk quickly to the front door. My boots are on the floor and my jacket is on a chair. I put them on quickly. I close the door behind me; luckily it self-locks. The mere thought of having to stay and face Jimena's family makes me feel sick to my stomach.

I walk downstairs and open the gate. I can feel the cold air nip my cheeks. This time I welcome it; it eases my headache. There is new snow on the ground. The whole world looks clean and bright. I used to hate snow back in Finland, but I'm learning to like it here. Snow slows the whole city down. It gives me space to breathe and think.

I walk to the bus stop. I hope a bus will arrive soon, but it's Christmas Day. It could be an hour or more before the next bus arrives. I look at the blinking Christmas lights someone has hung up on the windows across the street. I wonder if the people who live there are having a good Christmas. I hope they are.

We all wait for this one day, but it's not always as happy as we had hoped it would be; too many expectations can put too much pressure on any event. People work too hard to make everything perfect and when the day finally arrives, everyone's exhausted and cranky.

I remember Christmases when I was a child. I would get up before five and play in the living room, impatiently waiting for Christmas to happen. At three *joulupukki* arrived with his big bag of presents and the waiting was finally over. Soon after, the grownups would begin to argue and the magic was replaced with a sickening feeling of fear.

My first Christmas with Greg wasn't all that different. Halfway across the evening he began to sulk having read a text from Alene. He went to bed shortly afterward and left me alone at the dinner table. I began to think more and more that I had made a terrible mistake, but it was too late to do anything about it.

The bus arrives.

The driver looks sleepy. I feel sorry for him; he doesn't get to be with his family. Or maybe he doesn't have a family. Maybe he's just like me.

I find a seat and pull my phone from my pocket. Sara and Samuli have sent a video. They wish Greg and I Merry Christmas. I haven't told Sara the truth. I know I need to, but I just don't know how.

She told me not to marry him.

My cat welcomes me home. It tilts its head and looks at me as if asking if I had a good time. I wonder if it's glad to see me or if it's just hungry. I assume it's a bit of both.

"*Voi ei!* I forgot to bring you a treat! But you don't care, do you? Fish is all you want, isn't it?"

My cat follows me to the kitchen. I open a can of cat food and leave my cat to eat its food in peace.

I take a long hot shower. It makes me feel sleepy. It's a good thing. I have nothing to do other than sleep all day.

I get into bed; the sheets are cold. I pull the blanket all the way up to my chin, hoping my body will warm the bed up soon. My cat comes and lies down next to me. It eyes me as if waiting to see if I'll shoo it away.

"*Sä voit olla siinä.* You can stay, just this once."

I close my eyes.

Ensi vuonna Suomessa.

Next year in Finland.

18

I see Jimena walking briskly across the store. She stops in front of me.

"Marja! Where did you go? Everyone was so worried! I tried to call you a million times!"

"I went home," I say, staring at the people who have come to spend their last dollars before the year is over.

"Why? I wish you had stayed. *Abuela* made *menudo* for breakfast."

"I don't think I could have eaten anything."

"Did I give you too much to drink?" asks Jimena, biting her lower lip. "I just thought you needed it. I knew you were upset. I would have been upset too if my ex paraded his new girlfriend in front of me. He should have taken her somewhere else. Your ex is such a *pendejo*!"

"How did you know it was him?" I ask with a surprised look.

"You have a picture of him in your phone. I saw it when I looked for a photo of you for the Tinder app."

I look away for a moment.

"It wasn't a new girlfriend," I say quietly.

"Who was it then?" asks Jimena. Suddenly her eyes widen and she mouths "Oh my God!"

"It was his ex-wife, wasn't it? He brought her here so you could see them together. God, Marja! I knew he was mean to you, but that was just cruel!"

I continue to stare at the register. I'm used to Greg's cruelty. I'm surprised Jimena was able to see through him with such ease. Everyone else always thought he was so damn perfect. People congratulated me and said they envied me. They wouldn't have envied me if they had seen my favorite book in the bathtub. Greg threw it there when I didn't want to try some new thing he had seen in an X-rated movie. He turned on the faucet and held me by my neck and forced me to watch as the words blended on the wet pages. He said if he couldn't get what he wanted then neither would I.

"Are you okay?"

I glance at Jimena and force a smile.

"Yeah."

She presses her lips together for a moment. I can tell she's thinking.

"Pablo thought you were really cute. He said he understood why Jake liked you so much."

I can feel a smile appear. I know Jimena is trying to cheer me up.

"Oh, and Miguel asked about you."

I freeze.

I know that look on Jimena's face. It's one of conspiracy and amusement. She thinks this is funny.

I don't.

I know she means well, but I don't need any more complications. And I especially don't want her to remind me about Miguel. My knees become weak and my mouth feels dry when I think of him. I tell myself I'm being dumb. I don't know why he would be asking about me, not after the way I behaved. He's probably just being polite.

Jimena looks at her phone.

"I'll be right back," she says and walks toward the glass doors.

"Where are you going?" I call after Jimena.

She doesn't respond.

I look around frantically to see if a manager is anywhere nearby. I can't see one. Maybe she'll be okay. I hope so. If she gets fired I won't have anyone to talk to. I'll lose my only friend.

I hear someone coughing. I turn to look. A woman has dropped a sweater on the counter. She continues to stare at her phone; she doesn't look at me. I take the sweater and scan the barcode. I notice a little boy in the stroller next to the woman. I smile and wave at him. He smiles back at me. I fold the sweater and put it in a bag. The woman pays with a card, takes the bag and leaves without ever having looked at me. I don't know why people always talk about poorly behaving children. In my opinion, children behave so much better than grownups.

"*Hola,* Marja."

I turn and find myself looking into Miguel's soft eyes. Jimena joins me behind the service counter and gives me a bright smile.

"Marja, isn't it time for your break? Why don't you have coffee with Miguel?"

"Um, my break is only fifteen minutes."

"Then walk and talk," says Jimena, giving me another bright smile.

Right.

Walk and talk.

Just another oddity here.

I leave the register and walk with Miguel to the glass doors. We stand outside of the store for a moment. Miguel looks at me; his eyes are apologetic.

"I'm sorry. You really don't have to if you don't want to."

"It's okay, It's just—" my voice trails off.

"I get it. Jimena is always trying to set people up. I guess it's fun for her since Carlos isn't here. She misses him."

"I know. She talks about him all the time."

"Yeah, we know," laughs Miguel.

I stare at the floor for a moment.

"Coffee would be nice."

"Okay, well, let's get you some."

We walk to the coffee stand. I order black coffee, Miguel orders the same. He pays for both of our coffees. I want to say I can pay, but I'm grateful for the free coffee so I stay quiet.

"Jimena told me you're from Finland. What do you think of Chicago?"

I press my lips together. I don't know how to say any of it without sounding like I'm bashing the city and with it the whole country. Greg always told me I sounded ungrateful when I tried to explain how I felt.

"It's, um, interesting," I mumble.

"Interesting, huh?"

"I mean, it's nice, but…"

"…it's big and loud and it's driving you crazy."

I stare at Miguel. How did he know?

"It's what my friends who live out in the suburbs tell me when they visit. You had the same look on your face."

I sip my coffee and try not to look at Miguel. It's not about feeling awkward before strangers; not this time. I don't want to look at Miguel because I know my eyes reflect intense interest and I don't want him to see it.

"So, do you miss Finland?"

"I—"

I press my lips together and stare at my coffee. I don't want to answer that question either. It doesn't matter what I say, it sounds wrong every time.

"Sometimes," I say and blush mildly.

"I know what you mean."

I glance at Miguel. I've heard people say that so many times, but usually people don't have a clue. They just think they do.

Miguel laughs.

"Okay, you're right, I don't know what it's like to live in another country, but I do know what it's like to live in two cultures. When I visit my grandparents it's as if they never left Mexico. And every time I leave their house, it's like I'm entering another world. So yeah, I get it."

"It's just like that, but… I'm always in that other world."

"It must be hard for you to be here without your family."

I stare at my coffee again. Miguel glances at me. He must

have noticed I looked uncomfortable, because he changes the subject.

"So, what do you do when you're not working?"

"I like to read and go for walks."

"Good ways to spend your time."

I glance at Miguel again. I'm not sure he means it. Americans say a lot of things just to be polite.

"I, um, need to go back to work," I say, and motion toward the store with my hand.

"Okay, I'll walk you back," says Miguel and throws his coffee in the trash. He didn't take even one sip.

We stop by the glass doors.

"Thanks for the coffee," I say and smile.

"You're welcome. I—"

Miguel rubs his neck with his left hand. He looks indecisive for a moment.

"Um... Okay, full confession, I did ask Jimena if she could set this up. I just wanted to make sure you wanted to see me too. With Jimena you never know."

I bite my lower lip.

"Did she tell you I'm still married?"

"Yeah, she did."

"And that doesn't bother you?"

"It would, but she told me your husband is back with his ex. He left you, so you can do whatever you want now."

I glance at the people around us. For a moment I consider saying bye and walking away, but something in his eyes keeps me there. They reflect the same intense interest I know he can see in my eyes as well.

"I did want to see you too," I say, blushing again.

Miguel smiles.

"Do you have a phone?"

"Yes, of course," I say, laughing.

"What's your number?"

"It's—"

"Actually, give me your phone and I'll send myself a message, that way I'll have your number."

I hand my phone over to Miguel and watch as he types a message. He gives my phone back to me.

"Okay, well, I'll talk to you later," he says and raises his right hand to say bye. I smile and watch as he turns around and walks away.

I'm about to walk into the store when my phone beeps. I glance at the incoming text and almost drop my phone.

"I think you're gorgeous. Call me."

I look into the crowd. He's already vanished.

My heart pounds.

He called me gorgeous.

No one has ever called me gorgeous.

I see Jimena smiling like the sun behind the service counter.

"*So*…. What did you two talk about?"

"Nothing."

"Nothing?! *Ay,* Marja, I know you're lying! Miguel doesn't ever shut up! I know you talked about something."

I blush and look at the cash register.

"We talked about… life?"

"I bet you did," says Jimena with an enigmatic smile.

I turn to look at Jimena. She can read me like a book, but I can never tell what she thinks.

"Jimena, why did you leave the store earlier? You know you can get in trouble for that."

"Oh, don't be silly! I didn't leave the store! Miguel sent a message and told me he was in front of the store. I just went to get him. I did it for you! Aren't you happy?"

I turn to look at the register.

I don't know if I should thank her or chew her out. I know Jimena means well, but another relationship is the last thing I need right now. They always end and when they do I end up confused and alone. Besides, I'm going home soon. How could I possibly begin a new relationship now?

I smile at a customer and try not to think of Miguel and the way he looked at me, but I can't help it. I know he is interested in me. I have no idea why, but he is. And it wasn't just Jimena's idea this time. Maybe I could see him a few times before I go home. There's no real harm in that. I'm not going to marry him or become serious in any way. I just want to spend some time with him, that's all.

I smile at the thought.

Jimena was right about one thing.

It doesn't hurt to live a little.

19

I look at my reflection in the mirror. My skirt is too short, my shirt is too tight, and my heels are too high. This is what I get for letting Jimena dress me for the party.

"¡*Ay*, Marja! You look *fantastic*!"

I glance at Jimena. She's wearing a long white satin dress and her hair is pulled up. She looks like she's on her way to the Oscars.

"Are you sure you don't have a skirt that is a bit longer?"

"¡*Dios mio,* Marja! Don't you want to look nice? It's New Year's Eve!"

"I just don't know how I'm supposed to sit with this skirt."

"That's easy. Just keep your knees together."

I look at myself in the mirror again and try to hold in the sigh.

"Miguel is going to be there too," says Jimena with a teasing smile.

"I know. He told me."

"Oh, so you two have been talking?"

"A couple of times."

I don't want to tell Jimena that we've talked on the phone every day for the past five days.

It would be like throwing gasoline on a fire.

The club is packed.

Jimena sees her friends by the bar.

"Come! Let's get some champagne!"

I follow Jimena and wonder how much it will cost. It's exhausting to be poor, but it's so much worse to be hungry. If I'm not careful I won't eat for a week. Someone hands me a glass. I shake my head to say "no thanks."

"*Take it, it's already paid for*," whispers Jimena.

I take the glass and take a sip of the cold sparkling wine. It feels as if tiny pearls tickle my throat.

I turn and look around the room.

I see Miguel by the door.

He's looking at me.

He makes his way through the crowd without breaking eye contact with me. He puts his hand between my shoulder blades and kisses me on the cheek.

"*Hola, cariño*, you look beautiful tonight."

"Miguel!" calls Jimena. "Have you seen Pablo?"

"He's parking the car."

"¡*Ay*, Miguel! Did you make him the designated driver?"

"Hey, it wasn't my decision!"

Jimena waves her hand as to say "whatever."

I recognize the name. It's Jimena's brother. That means Jake could be here too.

I bite my lip.

"What's wrong?" asks Miguel, his eyes filled with concern.

"Oh… nothing," I say, trying to smile.

A moment later I see Jake in the crowd. The young

woman next to him could be Jimena's sister, except her complexion is darker; it makes her only look more striking. I feel as if I'm in a soap again, but this time I'm one of the plain extras, hired to make the stars look even more gorgeous.

Jake walks to the bar with his date. I follow him with my eyes. I hope he won't see or recognize me. Jake turns and looks at me. He tilts his head. I can tell he's trying to place me. The light returns to his eyes and a smile appears on his lips.

Shit!

Jake walks over to us and gives Miguel a side hug.

"Hey, man, it's been awhile."

"How was California?"

"Crowded," says Jake and laughs. He looks at me.

"It's Maria, right?"

"Marja."

"Right."

Miguel looks at both of us.

"You two know each other?"

"Yeah, we went out once before Christmas."

I stare at Jake. I'm not sure if I see amusement or sympathy in his eyes. He looks toward the bar and puts his hand on Miguel's left shoulder.

"I'll talk to you later, ok? You two have fun."

"Yeah, you too."

I can barely breathe. I don't want to look at Miguel. I don't want to know what he's thinking.

"It was Jimena's idea, wasn't it?" says Miguel without

looking at me.

"Yeah, it was. I mean, she made a Tinder account for me and—"

"She put you on *Tinder*?"

I turn to look at Miguel. He looks genuinely shocked.

"Did you want to be there?" he asks, looking at me with searching eyes.

"Not really, I—"

Miguel puts his glass on the counter.

"I'll be right back."

I watch as he walks over to Jimena. I see them having a heated discussion. I look around the room and wish I could just disappear. The only two people I know are arguing because of me. I hope at least one of them is going to talk to me tomorrow.

Miguel comes back.

"She won't meddle anymore," he says, grabbing his drink from the counter. His jaw is clenched and his eyes flicker. I watch as he finishes his drink in one quick sweep.

I turn my back to the bar.

I don't dare to look at Jimena. I don't want to know what she's thinking either.

I stare at the dancing people without seeing them.

I feel someone touching my arm. I turn my head and see Miguel. His eyes are soft again, almost apologetic.

"Would you like to dance?"

"Sure," I say and force a smile.

Miguel takes my hand and leads me to the dance floor just as the music changes to a slow song. He puts his arms around my waist and pulls me closer until our bodies touch. I place my hands on his shoulders. He smells just like he did at Christmas, but this time another scent is more pronounced; it's a mixture of whiskey and vanilla. We move slowly to the music. I can feel my whole body tingle as if every cell in my body has been awakened. I lean my head against his shoulder. I close my eyes. I feel as if I've come home from a long trip and I can finally relax—

I hear people stirring around us.

"Ten, nine, eight, seven, six, five, four, three, two, one, Happy New Year!!"

People begin to cheer. Black and gold balloons fly all around us. I look around the room and laugh. It's just like in the movies. I see Miguel looking at me; his smile is amused. I can feel my cheeks burn suddenly. I know I must have looked like this is the first time I've ever left the small town I was born in.

Miguel leans closer until he's close enough for me to hear him.

"Do you want to get out of here? There is a small place just around the corner. We can have a drink there."

"Okay, but I should probably tell Jimena."

"You can text her later, she's busy."

I glance at Jimena. She's surrounded by a crowd. I just hope I can find her later. All my things are still in her apartment.

I take Miguel's hand and follow him through the celebrating crowd.

He opens the front door for me.

The cold air feels good on my skin after the stuffy club. I step on the snowy sidewalk and nearly slip. Miguel grabs my arm.

"Are you okay?"

"Yeah, it's just that these shoes aren't meant for walking on snow and ice. I don't know why I let Jimena convince me to wear them."

"It's okay. We'll walk slowly."

Miguel puts his right arm around my waist. I take a few tentative steps and nearly slip again. I grab Miguel's left arm to steady myself. I get the feeling he enjoys being this close. I tell myself not to read too much into it.

We reach the bar and enter the small space.

It's quiet.

We sit down by the counter.

"What do you want to drink?" asks Miguel.

"Vodka with diet coke, thanks."

I look around the room while Miguel orders our drinks. The walls are covered with old photos. I feel as if I've been transported to the previous century. I don't know what the rest of the country is like, but I get the point that nostalgia is a big thing here. I turn to face the bar again and see my drink on the counter. I take a sip. It actually tastes decent. Miguel must have ordered a more expensive brand. It's not as clean as Finlandia, but it's not bad.

I stir my drink for a minute.

"Can I ask you something?"

"Yes, of course," says Miguel, taking sip of his whiskey.

"Have you always lived in Chicago?"

"Yeah, I was born here."

"Was Jimena born here too?"

"Yes, of course," says Miguel laughing as if I've said something amusing.

"Then I don't understand. You speak perfect English. Why doesn't Jimena?"

"Jimena does it on purpose. She speaks perfect English when she wants to. I told her once to stop pretending and she got mad at me and told me she's Mexican too and wants to sound like one."

"But doesn't it make people treat her badly?"

"Very few people treat Jimena badly."

I glance at Miguel. He has a strange look in his eyes, almost as if he disapproves of something. But I know what he means. I've noticed no one laughs at Jimena when she talks, not the way they do when I talk. They all smile and want her attention. It seems beautiful people get to do things the rest of us don't.

"What is it like in Finland? Do people treat you badly if you have an accent," asks Miguel, turning to look at me.

"They do, but at the same time we think it's a miracle if anyone learns Finnish."

"What do you mean?"

"It's just a really hard language to learn. We usually say we're sorry when someone says they are learning Finnish."

"You do? Wow, okay, I guess I'm not going to try it then," says Miguel, laughing.

I glance at him. I'm not sure why he would want to learn

Finnish, but I know it's hard to explain to someone whose language is perfect what it feels like to struggle with words; what it feels like when your words make you sound like you've never set a foot in a school building, when your IQ drops twenty points every time you open your mouth.

I decide to change the subject.

"Is it normal for people to give to strangers here? I mean, someone paid my bus fare the other day when I didn't have enough money on my card. I didn't even ask, she just did it."

"It's good karma."

"People believe in karma here?"

"Not everyone, but people like to give. It makes them feel good about themselves and it creates a feeling of community."

"But if they give because they want to community, why does everyone think they have to have a lot of money for themselves?"

"They think it'll make them happy."

"But it doesn't."

"You're right, it doesn't. But it's like with hungry people. They think having plenty of food will make them happy until they have had enough to eat. Then they realize there is more to life than food."

"So, the American Dream, it's about money?"

"It's about money now, but originally it wasn't. It was created when people had little and the dream was to have enough. Now it's about how much stuff you can buy that you don't need."

"Then I think the American Dream is the place where people throw their garbage. I mean, it's filled with stuff people don't need."

Miguel laughs out loud.

"You're smart, but I'm sure you already knew that."

I blush and stare at my drink. No one has ever called me smart. I've always felt I had to play dumb to be accepted.

"And you're right, the level of materialism we have here is ridiculous, but America isn't all bad. I mean, yes, it's superficial and driven by consumerism, but if you look underneath the surface, you find good people too. It's kind of like being on a cruise ship. You meet a lot of superficial people who just want to show off their money, but if you walk around long enough, you'll meet the ones who are there because they love the ocean."

I look at Miguel for a moment. I don't know why he called me smart. I've never heard anyone talk the way he does.

"How do you know so much?"

"Not every American is ignorant."

I can feel my cheeks flush again.

"I didn't mean it that way. You just know a lot."

"I like to read. We got a great library downtown. I'm sure you've seen it."

"No."

"Really? Well, I'll have to take you there sometime."

Miguel finishes his drink and glances at me.

"How long have you lived here now?"

"A little over a year."

"Have you had Chicago-style pizza yet?"

"I don't think so."

"Well, you have to try it! How about Thursday?"

"I can't— "

I see disappointment in Miguel's eyes.

"…afford it," I say and stare at my drink. I can feel the humiliation burn within.

"Hey, don't worry about it. It'll be my treat."

I look at Miguel. His eyes reflect the same gentleness I saw in them when he asked if I wanted to dance. He's the nicest person I know. Why couldn't I have met him two years ago instead of Greg? I glance at the clock on the wall.

"Oh, no! I forgot to text Jimena!"

"She'll get over it."

"No, you don't understand. All my things are at her place. My shoes, my clothes! My keys!"

"Oh, well, we better get you there then. I have a key to her place. I'll call a taxi."

I go to the bathroom and change my clothes. It feels good to get out of Jimena's clothes although I'm halfway glad I wore the skirt. I noticed Miguel admiring my legs a few times when he thought I wasn't watching.

"I think I got everyt—"

The door opens and Jimena stumbles in.

"Marja! I was wondering where you went! Hey, Miguel, can you help me out of this thing."

I watch as Miguel unzips Jimena's dress.

I stare at both of them. A couple of hours ago they were arguing. Now they are acting as if nothing happened.

"Marja, come, I need to talk to you."

I go to the bedroom after Jimena.

"Did you have a good time?" asks Jimena as she takes off her dress and puts on a T-shirt.

"I did."

"Good. Close the door."

I close the door and turn to look at Jimena who is removing her jewelry by the mirror.

"So, what do you think of Miguel? Do you like him?"

I try to think of a way to answer.

"If you don't, you better tell him now. He's already head over heels."

I look at Jimena with a confused look. I don't understand what she means.

"Head over heels, you know, in love with you."

"I don't think so," I blurt out, laughing.

"He's super protective of the woman he loves. He was mad at me because I created a Tinder account for you. He was jealous. He told me to stop setting you up."

I blush and look at the floor.

"So if you don't like him, now is the time to tell him."

I look at Jimena who has put on pajama pants and looks still just as gorgeous as she did before.

"I do like him, but—"

"No buts! Either you do or you don't!"

I look away for a moment. I don't know how to tell

Jimena I have no serious intentions, but I know I can only tell her what she wants to hear right now.

"I do."

"Good! Now, let's go find Miguel."

I follow Jimena to the living room. Miguel smiles when he sees me.

"Are you ready to go home?"

Jimena gives Miguel a look that tells him not to be absurd.

"Who needs to go home? It's New Year's Eve! Let's watch a movie!"

"It's getting kind of late, don't you think?"

"Late? It's not even three yet! We all have a day off tomorrow. Live a little, cousin!"

"Do you want to stay?" asks Miguel, looking at me.

"I can."

"See? You two choose a movie, I'll go make popcorn. And Miguel, no horror movies," says Jimena, giving him a look that tells him she means it.

"Yeah, okay."

I sit down on the couch. Miguel sits down next to me and turns on the TV. He scrolls through the movies.

"Does this sound good to you?"

I look at the title. I've already seen it.

"Yeah, sure."

Jimena returns with the popcorn. She looks around for a moment. She goes to the bedroom and brings two blankets.

"It's getting cold, yes?"

Jimena's apartment isn't exactly cold, but I don't say

anything. It feels good to have someone fuss the way Jimena does. I freeze when she spreads a blanket over both of us. I sit as still as I can and stare at the TV. I should've known Jimena had ulterior motives.

Ten minutes into the movie, Jimena grabs her phone and gets up.

"I'll be right back."

I can feel Miguel place his arm on the couch behind me. I glance toward the bedroom. I wonder if Jimena is coming back soon.

Our eyes meet.

I can see something tender in Miguel's eyes. He leans closer slowly as if giving me time to say no if I want to. He kisses me gently. His lips are soft; they fit mine perfectly.

I was right.

This is exactly what I need.

20

I stare impatiently toward the horizon.

"Come on, *come on*, show up!"

I wonder again why the bus is always late when I need it to be on time and on time when I'm late. I doubt Miguel is going to wait more than a few minutes.

Two minutes later I see the bright lights down the street. The bus stops in front of me with a screech. I press my card against the reader and take a seat at the back. I pull my phone from my pocket and think about sending a text to Miguel, but I'm not sure if it would sound too desperate. I may still be on time if the bus makes up lost time with less traffic.

I stare at the view outside the window without seeing anything. I think of the way Miguel kissed me on New Year's Eve. I've had my fair share of kisses, but there was something different about the way he kissed me. It was as if he actually saw me.

The bus moves along with the traffic. At Milwaukee Avenue I feel someone kicking my seat. I turn to look. I see a woman with a little girl.

"No, no, no, don't touch it!" says the girl, pulling her hand away.

"I'm not going to touch it, I just want to look."

"No!!"

"It looks okay, just some extra blood."

The little girl puts her hand on the string.

"I'm not pulling it," she says, smiling coyly.

The woman smiles and pulls her phone from her bag.

"Say cheese! Can you say 'cheese'?"

"Cheeeeeese!"

I glance at the woman who smiles encouragingly. Americans know how to give the gift of confidence to their children. Finnish parents weed out every notion of confidence as soon as possible. They know society requires conformity and an over-confident child won't get very far. It's not so much about not wanting their children to succeed as it is about a general dislike of anything excessive. Boasting about plenty inevitably invites disaster to equalize the lot; it is better to be humble than hungry even when hunger is no longer an issue.

I know how to be humble. I've never considered myself special in any way. It's probably why I didn't get anywhere in Finland. The weirdest thing is although Finns praise humility, they require excellence from everyone in all areas of life. Everyone has to be good at everything; they just can't talk about it. The expectations are so high most people are just happy remaining average instead of trying to excel beyond their abilities. I'm not sure which is better: to have so much confidence you think everything you do is great or to lack confidence to such a degree that you fear everything, even yourself.

I get off the bus and half-run down the street. I hope Miguel hasn't left yet. I see him waiting outside the pizzeria as soon as I turn the corner.

"I'm sorry I'm late," I say, adjusting my hat. "The bus was late."

"It's okay. Welcome to Chicago, right?" says Miguel laughing.

I take a deep breath and smile. Greg used to throw a complete hissy fit if I was late, even if it was only by a minute; he didn't have a similar rule for himself.

We enter the pizzeria. I let Miguel order. It's only fair in my opinion since he's paying. I don't know if this is a date or if we're just going out as friends. He didn't say and I didn't ask. I'm not sure how dating works in this country. I've never tried it.

We sit down by the window.

"Did you go the gym yesterday?" I ask, trying to sound lighthearted. I don't know how to do small talk, but I know I need to try.

"No, I decided to finish the book I've been reading for a few days."

"Oh, what was it about?"

"The history of ancient Mayans. It was from a different perspective, that's why I wanted to read it."

"You like reading history books?" I say with wide eyes.

"Of course!" says Miguel, laughing at my expression. "If you don't know where you've been, how can you know where you're going?"

"That's true."

"You don't like history?"

"Oh, I do, I just—"

I stop myself before I say I didn't think Americans did. It sounds rude even to me. I glance at Miguel.

"Can I ask you something?"

"Sure," says Miguel with a relaxed smile.

"Why are Americans either super happy or super unhappy? I mean, they either smile or they're mad or they cry. There's nothing in between."

"What are Finns like?" asks Miguel, laughing.

"Serious, I guess. People don't talk. I mean, women talk, especially about their feelings, men not so much."

"What about crying?"

"It's, uh, shameful? Especially in public."

"Why is it shameful?"

"Because you're supposed to control yourself, especially if you're a grownup."

"You don't cry at funerals?"

"Of course we do," I say, laughing. "It's okay to cry sometimes, but only if you have a really good reason."

"You don't think Americans have a good reason to cry?"

"I'm sure they do. But how can you smile, then cry, and then smile again?" I say, shaking my head.

"You get used to it," shrugs Miguel.

I give him a look that says I'm not so sure about it.

We sit in silence for a moment.

"There's another thing I don't understand. Why does everyone always want to know where I'm from?"

"Americans are nosy," says Miguel, laughing again.

"Yeah, I've noticed that. But I don't understand why they want to know. I mean, what are they going to do with the information?"

"I've never thought about it that way."

"I think they should ask only when they actually know you."

"I think that's a great plan," smiles Miguel.

"Me too. It would make me feel less like I'm an animal in a zoo."

"Is that how you feel?"

"Sometimes," I say, and glance out the window.

"That's not cool, but I know what you mean. I've heard my grandmother say something like that too."

"Your grandmother came from Mexico, right?" I say turning to look at Miguel again.

"Yeah, she did."

"I've noticed people don't like Mexicans here. Is it because you share a border?"

"Kind of. Mexico and the United States fought a war a long time ago and Mexico lost. It's been people against people ever since."

"Oh, that makes sense. Finns don't like Russians either because of the wars."

"It's complicated for sure."

"But I still don't understand why they dislike people who live *here*. Isn't everyone an American?"

"People like hierarchy. That way they can feel superior to everyone else without actually being any better."

"That's just like the Swedes. They don't like Finns."

"Why not?"

"I don't know. They just don't. My dad is from Sweden. I spent my summers with him when I was a kid. I could always tell people didn't like me because I was a Finn."

"Really? I thought all you Nordic people were friends."

"Yeah, no!" I say and laugh.

"So the Finns don't like the Swedes either?"

"Nope," I say and laugh again.

"People can be strange for sure. But in the end, life is what you make of it. If you let people get to you, they win."

I glance at Miguel. I know he's right, but it's not that easy to ignore when you've always been on the losing side.

The server brings the pizza and places it on the table between us.

Miguel places a slice on my plate. I smile and take a bite. I glance at the pizza. I'm not so sure what the excitement is all about. It's soggy as if someone has poured a whole can of tomato sauce on it and left it to drown.

Miguel gives me one of his amused looks.

"You don't like it?"

"It's…uh… different," I say and press my lips together. I don't know what to say without insulting him and everyone around us.

"What kind of pizza do you like?"

"Um… Italian?"

He looks at me with smiling eyes.

"Of course you do. I don't even know why I asked. You don't have to eat it if you don't want to."

"It's okay," I say and take another bite. The pizza could

be covered in anchovies and I would still eat it, I'm that hungry. I've been eating spaghetti with ketchup since I bought new shoes on Monday; I had ten dollars left for the rest of the week. I knew I shouldn't have bought them, but I couldn't meet Miguel looking the way I did. It was just too embarrassing.

I take a sip of my drink and glance at Miguel. He's the first person who has actually answered any of my questions. Jimena told me not to worry and Greg never explained anything. I'm sure Miguel finds my questions tiresome, but I just want to know how this country works. It would make my time here so much easier if I knew more.

"I have another question, if you don't mind."

"Go ahead," says Miguel and smiles encouragingly.

"Why do so few people here tell the truth? I mean, I've noticed everyone says everything is perfect all the time. It can't be true."

"Most people want to look better than they are."

"But if everyone knows it's a lie, what's the point?"

"There is no point, other than that everyone wants to believe what they say is true."

"I think it's better to tell the truth."

"I agree."

I glance at my phone.

Shit!

"I'm so sorry, but I have to go. I have to be at work in ten minutes."

"No problems. I'll walk you there."

We leave the pizzeria and walk down Michigan Avenue. We stop at the crosswalk and wait for the lights to change. Large snowflakes begin to fall from the sky. I look up and let the flakes fall on my face. They tickle as they melt.

Miguel takes my hand. I glance at him. He smiles at me. I return the smile.

Maybe this was a date after all.

We reach the entrance to the mall just in time. I turn to face Miguel.

"Thanks for the pizza."

"Thanks for the company," says Miguel with a smile. He leans closer and kisses me. "I'll call you later, okay?" he whispers.

I nod and smile.

I see Jimena behind the register. She's smiling. I'm wondering if she is ever going to stop finding all of this amusing.

"*So…* how was the pizza?"

"It was good."

"You hated it," says Jimena and laughs.

"Yeah, okay, it wasn't the best pizza I've ever had, but I had fun."

"So, Miguel is nice, yes?"

"Yes, he's nice," I say, blushing.

"Good," says Jimena and smiles the way she always does when she gets what she wants.

~~~

I run toward the bus stop.

The bus takes off.

I stop running and take a deep breath. I tell myself I'm being ridiculous. The next bus will come in fifteen minutes.

I can wait.

I stand by the bus shelter and look at the empty bench.

I remember the day in October after Greg had left. How I sat on the bench, feeling lonely and scared. I think of Miguel and a smile appears on my lips.

The next bus arrives.

I take a seat by the window. I stare at the view that has become so very familiar by now.

The bus stops at a light.

I see Miguel coming out of a bar.

I'm about to wave at him when I see the young woman in front of him turn around. I watch as Miguel kisses her.

For a moment I feel as if the whole world stops moving.

I get up quickly and move to the other side of the bus. I pull up my hood to hide my face. I don't want him to see me.

I close my eyes and dig my nails into my palms.

A lonely tear finds its way down my cheek. I wipe it away with an angry movement. I haven't felt like an idiot for a few weeks, but I feel like one now.

I don't understand why all American men lie and cheat. But a much better question is why I don't ever learn anything. Anyone else would have learned every possible lesson from being with a man like Greg, but I don't seem to have learned anything.

I stare out the window without seeing a thing. I know now Miguel didn't mean a word he said. He didn't think I'm beautiful. It was all a lie.

I lean my head against the window.

I feel tired.

So endlessly tired.

21

Jimena takes her place next to me. She smiles at a customer and turns to look at me.

"Miguel called me to ask if you're okay. He said you didn't answer your phone yesterday."

I evade Jimena's eyes. I don't want to tell her what I saw. Thankfully a customer shows up. The woman is the chatty kind. She tells me how she hopes the outfit will work with her new shoes since it's supremely important everything is perfect for her son's engagement party. They got engaged on New Year's Eve, but the party is this weekend. She shows me a picture of her son with his fiancé. I tell her they look beautiful together. The woman fans her face as if she is the blushing bride herself. I've noticed mothers are possessive here, especially of their sons. Greg's mother looked me up and down as if I was something the cat had dragged in when she met me the first time. She barely spoke to me the few times I saw her after that.

The woman pays and leaves, waving to me as she disappears into the crowd.

"Okay, what's going on?" asks Jimena, crossing her arms. She has dropped the accent; she sounds just as American as everyone else.

"Nothing."

"Don't give me that! I know something's happened! Yesterday you two were completely in love, and now you won't answer your phone. Does this have something to do with your ex? Is he back again?"

I stare at the register and bite my teeth together.

"Tell me!" demands Jimena.

"I… I saw Miguel yesterday on my way back home. He was… kissing another woman."

"What!?"

I glance at Jimena. Her eyes are blazing and her lips have formed a tight line. She turns to look to her right. I can tell she's seething.

"I'm going to talk to him."

"No! Please, don't! He doesn't know I saw him."

"All the more reason!"

"Jimena, please, don't! I don't want him to know!"

"Are you sure?

"I am."

She looks at me for a moment.

"Okay, if you're sure. I just can't believe it! Sometimes I wonder if he's not trying to be more American than the Americans," she says, shaking her head.

I don't know what she means and I don't want to know. Miguel was just another dream without a foundation. I'm okay with never seeing him again.

I leave the mall and begin to walk toward the bus. I see Miguel walking toward me in the crowd. He waves when he sees me.

I look around. I can feel my mind racing.

What is he doing here?

A split second later I realize Jimena must have given him my schedule. It's not the first time I want to chew her out, but it's the first time I'm seriously wondering why she can't just mind her own business.

"*Hola,* Marja."

Miguel tries to kiss me. I turn my head away.

"What's wrong?"

"How can you ask that?" I retort angrily. I try to pass him but he moves in front of me.

"What are you talking about?"

"I saw you yesterday. You were with another woman."

"Yeah, so?"

"I don't believe this! You're all the same!" I exclaim out of sheer anger and frustration. I try to pass him again.

Miguel grabs my arm.

"Hey! Can we talk about this?"

"Let me go!"

He lets go off my arm and puts his hands up in the air.

"We never talked about not seeing other people."

I look at Miguel as if I don't understand what he's saying.

"If you didn't want me to see other women, you should have said so, I would have agreed."

I continue to stare at Miguel as if he's talking in a language I don't understand.

"Why do I have to tell you that? Isn't it obvious?"

Miguel laughs mildly.

"No, it isn't."

"You mean you think it's okay to date several people at the same time?"

"Yeah, everyone does it."

"It's insane!"

"Why is it insane?"

"Because you're promising the same thing to several people."

"It's not about promising anything, it's about keeping your options open, seeing who you like."

"I'm an option?" I say, not even trying to hide my disgust.

"Everyone is. You go out a few times until you decide who you want to be exclusive with."

"Exclusive?"

"Yeah, you know, you date only that person."

"I thought we were already doing that."

"Hey, I didn't make the rules," says Miguel, laughing again.

I shake my head.

"I don't think this is going to work."

I turn around and begin to walk away. Miguel runs after me and places himself in front of me.

"What do you mean?"

"I don't think I can trust you."

Miguel exhales forcefully.

"Listen, I had no idea you didn't know about this. Besides, I was going to ask you last night if you wanted to be exclusive. I tried to call you five times, but you didn't answer."

"If you wanted to ask me that, why did you go out with that other woman?"

"It was arranged before I met you. She went to see her family for Christmas and we agreed we were going to meet after that. Besides, nothing happened. I just kissed her good night—after I told her about you."

I look at Miguel. I want to believe him, but I don't know if I can. The memory of Greg's betrayal is still with me.

I stare at the passing cars.

Miguel takes a step closer. He tilts his head and seeks eye contact. When I refuse to look at him, he places his hand on my right cheek and moves my head until our eyes meet. His eyes are serious.

"I will never hurt you, I promise."

I see something intense in his eyes. It's not just sincerity. It's desire—naked raw desire, for me. No man has ever looked at me that way. He places his arms around my waist and kisses me gently at first, then with more intensity. I can feel my knees give way. I put my arms around his shoulders to steady myself. I feel as if I'm becoming unglued at the same time as my heart is being glued back together.

Miguel leans his head back until he can see my eyes again.

"So… Marja *y* Miguel. It's poetic, yes?"

I try to think of something to say, but I can't think of anything. I can only smile.

Miguel pulls away and puts his hands in his pockets.

"Isabella is throwing a party tomorrow. Do you want to come?"

The question brings me back to reality.

"Is that your party cousin?"

"You've heard of her?"

"Jimena told me."

"Of course she did. Yes, Isabella likes to party more than all of us together, but her parties are always fun. So, you'll come?"

"Sure."

"Great! I'll pick you up around seven. Can you text me your address?"

"I can take the bus, it's no problem."

Miguel shakes his head and mouths "no."

"If you tell my cousin you took the bus, she's going to tell me I don't know how to treat women and I'll never hear the end of it."

I laugh and pull my phone from my bag. I type my address and hit send.

Miguel looks at me with a relaxed smile.

"Hey, do you want to have lunch with me? I have an hour before I have to be back at work."

"Sure, as long as it's not too expensive, I think I have five dollars—"

Miguel looks at me as if to ask "what's this?"

"I asked you out. I'll pay. Or is this something strange too?"

I look at my shoes. I feel like a duckling in a pond filled with swans.

"No, I just forgot."

"You mean men don't pay in Finland?"

155

"They do sometimes."

Miguel gives me a look that says he's sure I'm lying.

"You're serious? Okay, wow! But we better get going. If we stand here any longer we'll freeze to death."

I take his hand and smile.

A small voice reminds me I promised to keep it casual. This isn't keeping it casual.

I tell the voice to shut up.

22

Isabella opens the door. She smiles when she sees Miguel.

"¡*Hola,* Miguel!"

Miguel gives Isabella a kiss on the cheek.

"¡*Hola,* Isabella! This is Marja."

"¡*Hola,* Maria! ¡*Bienvenidos*¡ Welcome!"

I want to tell her my name is Marja, but I let it slide.

We walk into the living room where people are already dancing and drinking. Jimena sees us, stretches her arms above her head and makes a squealing sound. She looks elated as if she's already had a few drinks. Miguel looks at me and smiles. I can tell he thinks the same as I do.

"My two favorite people!" says Jimena and gives both of us a hug. "Are you two hungry? There is food in the kitchen."

"Can we get something to drink first?" asks Miguel, not even trying to hide his smile.

"Of course you can! *Pablo*!"

Jimena's brother looks up and waves at us.

"Pablo will make you whatever you want," says Jimena and returns to the impromptu dance floor in the middle of the living room.

I watch as Miguel goes to the corner of the room and talks to Pablo. I stand by the doorway and look at the people who are dancing. Their smiles are genuine, as if they are truly enjoying life. The people I met in Spain had the same relaxed look as if life was there to be lived instead of endured. I don't know what their secret is, but they are so different from the people I knew in Finland and the people I see at the mall here. They're all so tense I sometimes wonder if they all think they are participating in a pageant that has only a few winners and they are afraid it won't be them.

Miguel hands me a beer and takes my hand. I follow him to the kitchen and see the food on the counter. Just seeing it makes my stomach contract from hunger pains. I had nothing to eat this morning. I've been hungry before, but being hungry without being on a diet is one of the worst feelings in the world. It's as if you're just under the surface, trying to get up to breathe while every movement makes you only sink further. But I'm a guest so I have to show restraint. I can't repeat Christmas Eve no matter what.

Miguel gives me a plate and tells me to help myself. I place a tamale on the plate and step to the side.

"Oh, come on, you have to eat more! Why do you women always think you have to be so skinny?"

I feel my eyes become round from surprise. Greg always said I was getting chubby and I knew it was true. There's something about American food that just packs the pounds on you. I eat less here than I did in Finland, but I weigh more. At the same time I knew Greg said it to hurt my feelings. I give Miguel a quick smile and fill my plate.

I lean against the counter and take a bite of the tamale. It doesn't taste like the food you get at most restaurants here;

it doesn't taste plastic and bland. I don't know what they've put in it, but it tastes like love has been added as an extra ingredient. I know it's true, because it tastes a lot like the food my grandmother used to cook. I stare at the plate for a moment; I can feel my eyes misting. It's been so long I've felt at home anywhere. It's been equally long since I've felt truly loved by anyone. And here I am, at a party, surrounded by people who clearly care about me, eating food made with love. Who needs to win the lottery when you can have this?

I see Jimena coming to the kitchen. She looks around as if she's looking for something. Pablo comes after her.

"I told you! There are no more limes!"

"I thought there were."

"Did you go to the store like I asked you to?"

Pablo rubs his neck and stares at the floor.

"How could there be more limes if you didn't buy them, *estupido!*" exclaims Jimena and swats Pablo's arm.

"Okay, okay, I forgot!"

"You always forget! How does your wife live with you? Do you forget her too?"

"Hey, don't talk about my wife!" says Pablo giving Jimena a look that tells her to watch it.

"No, *she's* a good woman. You just can't focus for five seconds! I don't know how she puts up with you!"

Miguel looks at both of them. He laughs and shakes his head.

"Hey, Jimena! Let your brother be, okay?"

Jimena gives Miguel a frustrated look and spreads her

arms.

"We have no more limes!"

"They can drink without the limes! Just go enjoy the party."

Jimena gives Miguel another frustrated look and crosses her arms.

"Fine!"

I watch as Jimena leaves the kitchen. For some reason she listens to Miguel far more than she listens to her own brother. I'm not sure where the dynamic comes from. Maybe it's the close proximity of their ages that has created their special bond; they're both almost twenty-seven.

I finish eating and put my plate in the sink.

"Are you done?" asks Miguel with a smile.

I nod.

"Let's go to the back, we can talk there."

We enter a bedroom and sit down on the bed. The walls are pink and a set of Christmas lights hang on the wall above the mirror. It's clearly a girl's room, but it looks like it belongs to a teen instead of a little girl judging by the clothes that are scattered on the chair and the floor.

"Are you enjoying the party?" asks Miguel with a smile that seems oddly nervous.

"I am," I say and smile.

I notice he's fidgeting. I'm not sure why he's so nervous. He's usually just as confident and self-assured as everyone else although he has a gentle side too. I can see Miguel glancing at me a few times. He bites his lower lip as if he's trying to decide something.

Our eyes meet.

I can see the same intense desire returning to his eyes. He cups my right cheek with his left hand and kisses me gently. His kiss becomes hungry quickly. He lays me down. I can feel his hand travel down my body. His touch is gentle even when its firm. He kisses my neck and slips his hand under my sweater.

The door opens suddenly.

I see Jimena. She is about to walk into the room with her phone when she stops abruptly. The surprise in her eyes gives way to delight. She looks at me and puts her right index finger against her lips. She takes a step back and closes the door behind her.

Miguel raises his head and looks at me. He's breathing heavily and his face is flushed.

"Who was that?"

"Jimena."

Miguel looks confused for a moment. He lowers his head until it rests against my shoulder. I can hear him laughing. He sits up and slides his fingers through his hair.

"This is probably not the best place for this," he says, still laughing. "Maybe we should go somewhere else."

I sit up and slide myself to the edge of the bed until my feet touch the floor.

I look at Miguel. He's completely relaxed.

My throat constricts suddenly. It's not as if I don't want the same, but what if he'll think I'm cheap like Greg did?

Greg used to remind me that I slept with him the first night especially when he became angry. He told me he knew I was cheating on him because of it, that I was giving it to the whole neighborhood when he was at work. I wanted to ask him if it meant he was cheating on me too since I wasn't the only one in my bed that night, but I knew if I had asked him that he would only have begun to yell at me like he always did. I know Miguel is nothing like Greg, but I don't want Miguel to think the same.

He takes my hand when he sees the look on my face.

"Hey, it's okay. It was just Jimena, she doesn't care."

I stare at the floor. I can feel my cheeks burn. Slowly the realization Jimena isn't the reason for my silence reaches Miguel. He presses his lips together and looks away briefly. I can see him mouthing "fuck!" When he turns to look at me, his eyes are filled with regret.

"I didn't mean to… we can wait."

He gets up and pulls me up by my hand.

He brushes my hair from my face and for a moment he looks at me with serious eyes.

"I'm sorry, forgive me."

"It's okay. I just—"

I pause.

How can I explain his opinion of me matters more than anything else at this moment? I don't know how American men think. I have only Greg to go by and I don't think he was a very good example.

"I just don't want you to think that I—"

I look away. I don't know how to say it.

Miguel's eyes narrow. He looks at me as if he's trying to figure out what I'm getting at. A second later he leans his head back and makes a "mmm" sound as the thought comes to him. His eyes soften.

"I don't know what other people have told you," he says as he moves closer. "But I only have beautiful thoughts about you."

He puts his right hand behind my neck and wraps his left arm around my waist.

"And I will only have beautiful thoughts about you, because I love you," he whispers.

His words startle me. I look him in the eyes. I see sincerity and tenderness, and something I've never seen in anyone's eyes before. I see surrendering love. The room disappears and time stands still as I gaze into his eyes. A warm feeling fills me.

"I love you too," I whisper.

Miguel smiles and kisses me. I wrap my arms around his neck and close my eyes.

A small voice tells me this is going too fast.

I ask the voice if twenty-four years is too fast.

I've been waiting for this my whole life.

23

I see Miguel walking across the store. He smiles at me and continues to walk past the service counter.

The manager gave me a hard time yesterday when she saw Miguel talking to me by the register. She said I should leave my personal life at home. I nodded and swallowed. I can't lose my job. I'll become homeless if I do. I can't seek any assistance in any form for five years. Greg is supposed to support me. He signed an affidavit of support promising to do so. But he's gone now and so is his money.

I see the floater walking toward me. She stops next to me and gives me an annoyed look when I don't leave immediately. I give her a brief smile and leave the register. I walk toward the glass doors; I feel someone taking my hand. I leave the store and take a few steps to the side.

"I didn't get you in trouble this time, did I?" asks Miguel with a smile.

"No, we're okay," I say with a shy smile. I'm not used to this much attention.

"Do you want get some coffee?"

"Sure," I say. I can feel my cheeks flush again. I wish I could stop this infernal blushing, but I can't help it. Just being near Miguel makes me all warm and tingly.

We walk to the coffee stand. Miguel orders coffee for both of us. I smile when I notice he remembered I drink my coffee black.

"So, what's going on in the sordid world of retail?" asks Miguel as he hands a paper cup to me.

"Nothing," I say and laugh.

"I hope they're treating you right."

I look at Miguel. There it is again, that same look he had on New Year's Eve when I told him about the Tinder account Jimena had created for me. He's not considering what other people think of me; he's thinking what I think of other people.

"I don't think they even notice me most of the time."

"How can someone not notice you?" says Miguel, giving me a look filled with disbelief. I want to tell him it's easier than he thinks, but I just smile. I know he's giving me a compliment.

I sip my coffee and glance at Miguel a couple of times. He's staring at me without a hint of embarrassment. The way Americans are able to stare at people without averting their eyes is mystifying. I guess their ancestors didn't fear the evil eye or whatever it is Finns fear. I can only look someone in the eyes for a couple of seconds before I have to avert my eyes.

"When does your shift end?"

"Noon. I'm only working the morning shift today."

"Great! Would you like to go have some fun after that?"

"Sure…" I say and glance at the scene outside the mall. It's colder than cold although the sun is shining. The thought of spending the whole day outside isn't exactly appealing.

Miguel laughs when he sees the look on my face.

"Don't worry! We'll spend most of the time inside."

"Oh, in that case, sure!"

"Awesome! See you soon," he says and kisses me.

I watch as he leaves the mall. I feel all warm and tingly again. How incredibly easy it is to be with someone who actually cares.

We exit the train and take the escalator to street level.

"I hope you like art," says Miguel as we cross the street.

I look at the imposing building ahead of us. I see two green lions standing by the stairs. They look stern, as if they're keeping watch over all the priceless artworks inside. They remind me of Stockholm and all of its statues and rooftops made green by time and oxygen. I never thought I would miss that city, but I guess time changes us too.

"Hey, we should take a picture of ourselves with one of the lions!" says Miguel with excitement. "Come!"

I try to say I don't think it's such a good idea, but Miguel just laughs. He pulls me to himself and tells me to smile. He gives me a quick glance and tickles me to get me to smile as he takes the picture.

"See? I knew we would look great together," he says giving me his phone.

I look at the photo. For a moment I can't believe I'm looking at myself. My eyes shine and my smile is relaxed even as I'm trying to get away from being tickled. I cover my mouth with my mitten-covered hand to prevent myself from laughing out loud out of sheer surprise. I didn't even know it's what I look like at the moment. All I've known for months is the sad face I've seen in the mirror every morning.

I give Miguel his phone back and follow him up the stairs. We enter the warm building. I feel a sudden twinge of guilt. I know I should tell him I'm returning to Finland in a few months, but I don't know how to have the conversation with him. Besides, I'm sure this is nothing more than a fling for him. Jimena told me Miguel has never had a serious girlfriend. I know he said he loves me, but I'm sure he says that to every woman he meets. He's most likely going to be relieved when I leave.

A small voice tells me I won't be.

I ignore it.

24

I leave the store and walk down the wide walkway. I look at the items on display behind the windows as I pass the stores. I've never understood why some people feel the need to spend hundreds of dollars on a piece of fabric just to make themselves feel more important. There is always someone else who has spent more money on their clothes. It's a pointless competition.

I see Miguel waiting for me by the entrance. He hugs me and leaves his right arm around my waist. He seems to like doing it. I don't mind. It makes me feel protected. Back in Finland I would have laughed at the thought of someone having to protect me. After two months alone in this city I'm more than okay feeling protected.

We leave the mall together and walk down Michigan Avenue. I wonder where we're going. It's almost seven and it's already dark; there aren't that many places we could visit this late, unless he wants to take me out to dinner.

We stop at the bus shelter by Chicago Avenue. I glance at Miguel. He seems oddly tense. I wonder if he's just going to take me home. He's done that a couple of times this week just to spend time with me, but he picked me up with his car those times.

Miguel turns and looks at me.

"Would you like to come to my place?"

I see a strange mixture of eagerness and shyness in his eyes. I know why we're taking the bus. He wanted to give me an opportunity to go home alone if my answer was no.

"Sure," I say and blush.

"Great! I'll make us dinner."

"You know how to cook?" I ask, my eyes filled with surprise.

"Yeah, my mom taught me. She told me I shouldn't expect a woman to cook for me," laughs Miguel. "I don't know if she thought I was going to be single for life or if she was just tired of doing all the cooking herself."

I want to tell him I doubt very much his mom thought he would be single for life, but I'm beginning to understand why Miguel is so different from all the other men I've met. He doesn't treat me like I'm there to serve him. He sees me as an actual person. Most men say it's how they see women until it's dinner time.

Miguel opens the front door to his apartment.

I take off my shoes and hang my jacket on the coat rack. I walk into the living room. I look around. Miguel's apartment is immaculate, much cleaner than mine. I see several bookshelves filled with books. He wasn't joking when he said he liked to read.

"Do you want something to drink?"

"Sure."

I walk to the window and look out. He doesn't live that

many miles from me, but the view is so very different. The streets are clean here and a feeling of peace hovers over the neighborhood.

Miguel returns from the kitchen with two beers.

"How long have you lived here?"

"About three years."

"It's nice."

"Thanks. Hey, make yourself at home. I'll be in the kitchen for a bit."

"I can help," I say with far more eagerness than I had intended.

"Yeah? Okay, well, great!"

I glance at Miguel. His eyes reveal he's pleased. He's used every excuse in the book to see me all week and he's called every night. It's as if he can't bear the thought of being apart.

I follow Miguel to the kitchen. He pulls a few plates from the fridge.

"Do you want to cut the cilantro?"

"I can."

He pulls a cutting board from a drawer and gives me a knife. I cut the herb into thin slices. I glance at Miguel who is mixing ingredients by the stove. He has a focused, yet relaxed expression on his face. I've never met anyone who can focus as well as he does. I've seen him maneuver the CTA without losing his cool and he never gets mad while driving although most people in this city drive as if they were on a racetrack without rules.

I let Miguel know I'm done. He smiles and asks me to

bring the cutting board to the counter. He divides the chicken into two equal pieces and places them carefully on top of the rice. He smothers the chicken with a sauce and sprinkles the cilantro over it. He grabs both plates and motions with his head for me to follow him to the living room.

I sit down by the table. Miguel lights a candle and sits down on the opposite side.

"I hope you're hungry," he says and smiles.

I want to say I'm always hungry, but I know it would sound odd. I take a bite of the chicken. It's plump and flavorful. It's nothing like the dry chicken I sometimes buy from the store.

"What do you do again?" I ask and take a sip of my beer.

"I work in telecommunications."

"Do you like it?"

"It's okay, pays well."

"I wish I could say the same about my job."

"Yeah, retail isn't exactly the best-paying job in this town," says Miguel, laughing.

"No, it isn't," I say and laugh too.

"What would you like to do instead?"

"I'm not sure. I wanted to study biology, but I didn't get into the university when I applied, so that was that."

"Why not?"

"You have to, how do you say it, earn it?"

"Oh, it's merit-based."

"Yes, you have to have really good grades. Mine weren't good enough."

"*You* didn't have good enough grades?" says Miguel, giving me a look that tells me he's sure I'm lying.

"You have to have an almost perfect medium grade. I got a couple of eights, so no university for me."

"Wow! That sounds harsh."

"It's a small country. The government pays, so they only accept as many students as they feel they need to."

"Couldn't you have studied something else?"

"I didn't know what else I wanted to study."

"But can't you study biology now that you're here? I mean, there are plenty of schools in Chicago. I'm sure one of them would be more than happy to admit you."

I give Miguel a brief smile. I wouldn't be able to afford it even if I wanted to. I glance around the room to find something else to talk about.

"How did you find all of these books?"

"Oh, I've been buying books here and there. I've gotten rid of plenty over the years. Right now I'm just trying to keep the ones I like. You can borrow one if you want. You said you liked to read, right?"

"I do," I say and smile.

Miguel glances at me. I can tell he's thinking.

"Have you been anywhere other than Chicago yet?"

"No. I mean, unless the airport in New York counts?"

"Not exactly!" says Miguel, laughing. "Okay, when's your birthday?"

"Twelfth of April."

"In three months? We're going to have to celebrate! Where would you like to go?"

"Um… I don't know," I say carefully.

"It's okay. We've got time to think about it."

I glance at Miguel. Why is he talking about the future? A split second later I tell myself to stop being silly. This is what Americans do. Jimena explained it to me finally after I pestered her long enough. Americans talk about all the things you'll do together, but when the time comes they act as if they've never said anything. It's just part of the social game everyone participates in. It doesn't mean anything.

I follow Miguel to the kitchen.

"That was really good, thank you."

"Thanks for the help," says Miguel, giving me a kiss. He puts the plates in the sink and opens the fridge.

"Do you want another beer?"

"Sure."

Miguel hands me a bottle. I follow him back to the living room and sit down next to him on the couch.

"Do you want to watch something?"

"Yeah, sure."

I pull my legs up on the couch. It's getting late, but I don't want to leave yet. It's obvious Miguel doesn't want me to leave either. He wouldn't have suggested a movie if he did. I'm wondering if he's thinking the same as I am. I'm scared of a lot of things in life, but sex isn't one of them. I have been thinking about his body all week and it has occupied my thoughts far more than it should have.

Miguel chooses a movie and throws the remote on the table. I can see he has left his beer on the table.

I turn to look at him.

Our eyes meet.

I recognize the look in his eyes. They reflect what I know he can see in my eyes too. I put the bottle on the table and place my right hand behind his neck. I kiss him softly at first, then with more intensity. I can feel his hands begin to pull my shirt up impatiently; it's as if he's waited far too long and he can't wait a moment longer. I lean back and let him pull my shirt over my head; it lands on the floor. I unhook my bra and throw it on the floor too. He leans me down on the couch. I place my hand behind his neck again and pull him closer until I can kiss him. I can feel his hands on my body; they slide up and down my skin as if he wants to feel every part of me. I slide my hand down his back and begin to pull his shirt off. He leans his weight against his elbows; I pull his shirt over his head. He wrestles his shirt off one arm at the time. I kiss him again. My kiss is just as hungry as his; I want to taste him, feel him. His hands move down my body and find my waist. He pulls my jeans off just as impatiently as he removed my shirt. I begin to pull his jeans off. He slides them off until they are down by his ankles; he kicks them off. I can feel him kissing my neck. He slides his hands underneath my head. The rest of the world disappears when I feel him inside me. I kiss him and wrap my arms around his shoulders. I can feel his body move against mine as if we were born to meet each other halfway. He lifts his head and looks me in the eyes.

"*Eres la mujer más hermosa del mundo… te amo.*"

I feel I'm drowning in his eyes again.

"*Mä rakastan sua,*" I whisper.

I never knew it was possible to merge with someone so completely.

25

I wake up to music.

For a moment I wonder where I am. After a few seconds I realize I'm in Miguel's bedroom. I can hear him singing along to a song; his voice is melodious and soft.

I get up and look for my clothes. A moment later I remember they are still in the living room. I wonder if I should wrap myself in the sheet, but that would just look silly. I look into the closet and find one of Miguel's sweaters. I put it on and go to the bathroom. I see a toothbrush in a cup. I know I should brush my teeth, but I can hardly use Miguel's brush. I open a drawer and find a toothbrush still in its plastic casing. I tell myself I will him buy a new one later and open it.

The toothpaste feels cool in my warm mouth. I don't wonder it feels that way. We made love all night; we got barely two hours of sleep. I should feel tired, but instead I feel as if I've slept all of my life and I've finally woken up.

I go to the living room and find my underwear and socks. I place the rest of the clothes on the couch and go to the kitchen.

I see Miguel by the stove. I watch as he stirs vegetables in a pan and continues to sing. Spanish is like Italian; it's a smiley language. No one can say "*Andiamo!*" or "*Prego!*"

without looking like they're smiling. Finnish is expressive, but it doesn't translate into expressiveness. Finns sound as if they're arguing even when they're having a good time.

I walk over to Miguel and hug him from behind. I lean my head against his back. I love feeling his body against mine. It's comforting and sensual at the same time. Miguel turns his head and tries to make eye contact with me.

"Good morning, *mi amor*. Are you hungry?"

I let go off Miguel and move to the side. I look at the two plates. I don't usually eat breakfast, but the food looks delicious.

"No, but I can eat."

"You *can* eat? You should eat! Food is important!"

"What about love?" I ask with a teasing smile.

"Yes, love is very important. And so are you," he whispers and leans closer to kiss me. I grab his neck with my right hand and kiss him deeply. I pull away and look at him breathlessly for a moment. I don't even know where that came from. Miguel looks at me with surprise. A split second later a smile rises up to his eyes.

"I like a woman who knows what she wants," he says with a wink.

I press my lips together to hide a smile. Greg would have told me I was acting like a whore and told me to stop. He couldn't stand it when I took the initiative. He told me it wasn't what women were supposed to do.

But that's all gone now. I don't need to think about it anymore.

∽⌒⌒⌒

I stand by the kitchen counter and watch as Miguel washes the dishes. I said I could help, but he just shook his head and said he got it. He turns and smiles at me. Suddenly I see panic in his eyes.

"Wait! You drink coffee in the mornings, don't you? I didn't—I mean, I knew about it—I just didn't—"

"Don't worry, I can get it later," I say and smile.

I found out Miguel doesn't drink coffee two days ago. I was wondering why he always threw his coffee in the trash. I asked him about it and he gave me an almost embarrassed smile. He said it felt too obvious that he just wanted to see me unless he bought the coffee. I told him he should stop being silly, that he could come and see me whenever he wanted.

"I'll buy a coffee maker today, I promise."

I just smile. The panic leaves his eyes and the relaxed smile returns as he reaches for the kitchen towel.

"So, what should we do today?"

"You said something about the library in the city, the big one?"

"Yeah? You want to go there?"

"It was just an idea," I say, shrugging.

"It's actually a great idea. I have some books I need to return. Okay, well, let's go take a shower."

"Together?"

"It saves water," says Miguel with a sly smile and takes my hand.

178

We enter the library and walk down the hallway. I look around. The floors are covered with marble and a water fountain is placed next to the escalator. I feel as if I've traveled back in time and I'm in old Rome. It's the same feeling I had when I walked into the mall the first time. So much of this city reminds me of old Rome. I'm not an expert on the subject, but I've read enough to see the similarities. The class system is alive and well, as are the imperial baths; they've just been replaced by shopping centers where the wealthy spend their days entertaining themselves while the poor toil away for wages that are barely enough to sustain life. The library is an oddity as it invites everyone in. Everyone can read for free. It's probably why most people don't. It doesn't give them the feeling of importance the way shopping does.

I hear my phone beep. I pull it from my pocket and look at the incoming text. The whole room begins to spin around me.

It's Antero.

He wants to talk.

I stare at my phone. I don't know what he wants to talk about and I really don't want to know. I can't imagine anything he has to say will excuse what he did. If I've learned anything from my time with Greg is that you don't just leave if you love someone. You stay and talk it out. Antero has had more than two years to contact me if he wanted to and he never did. Why does he want to talk now?

The sound of another incoming text startles me.

It's Sara.

She tells me she met Antero the previous night at a work function. He asked if she had my new phone number as my old number no longer works. She said she gave it to him. I send a quick thank you to Sara. The realization Antero tried to call me fills me with a sudden warm feeling. The feeling evaporates when I realize he waited more than a year to call. I didn't change my number until I moved here. Why did he wait that long?

"Are you okay?" asks Miguel, looking at me with concern in his eyes.

I look up.

"Yeah... I'm fine, um, Sara just sent a message."

"That's your friend, right?"

"Yes, she's my best friend in Finland."

"Okay, well, go ahead and talk to your friend. There's no rush, I'll wait."

I smile at Miguel and look at my phone again. I know I need to respond to Antero. I just don't know how to say what I need to say. I already know if I say the wrong thing, he'll clamp down and I'll never find out what happened. I need to move carefully just as I would if I was testing the first ice of the season. Some things just take their own time and can't be rushed no matter what. If I've learned anything during my time here is that haste makes waste. It's the equivalent of *"hijaa hyvää tulee."*

Sometimes Finns actually agree with Americans.

26

I help Jimena put the hangers away. I wonder why she seems so subdued. I want to ask her what's wrong, but I know she'll tell me when she's ready. It's not as if Jimena has a problem talking.

I feel my phone in my pocket. The new message from Antero is still there. I haven't read it yet although it's been five days since he sent it. I know I have to read it, but I dread it. What if he actually had a good reason to leave me?

No!

He left me without an explanation. He should have told me why he left; he should have given me a reason. Everyone deserves an explanation no matter how painful it is. It's better to hear the truth than be left wondering.

I see Jimena wiping her eyes.

"What's wrong?"

"Nothing."

I give Jimena a look that tells her I know she's lying.

"It's just that… I just can't stand this endless waiting anymore. What if Carlos can't ever come here? What am I going to do then? What if I don't want to move to Mexico? I know I said I would, but my family is here. I don't know if I can choose between my family and my husband. I mean, how did you do it?" asks Jimena, wiping her eyes again.

"I didn't think I was going to miss my family as much as I do," I say quietly.

"Yeah, we never do, do we? I mean, I didn't think I was going to miss my family when I went to Guadalajara. A year isn't that long, right? But I did miss them, I even missed Pablo! I mean, he drives me crazy more than not, but I actually missed him!" says Jimena, laughing.

"Why did you go to Mexico for a year?"

"Oh, I was doing some modeling jobs for a swimsuit company and I decided to stay for a bit after I met Carlos."

"I knew it!" I gasp. "I knew you could pose!"

Jimena blushes slightly.

"I don't ever talk about it. It was just something I did because it was easy money. I should have quit earlier than I did. It was all so superficial. I felt like I was a brainless doll someone else was directing most of the time. In the end I couldn't stand it."

"But I bet it paid well."

Jimena laughs again.

"A lot better than this job!"

"I really hope Carlos can come here soon," I say and give Jimena a consoling smile.

"Me too," she says and stares at the register.

For a moment she has the same look in her eyes I can only imagine I've had a dozen times or more. Jimena is gorgeous and the whole world loves her, but there are moments when we're all equal in our desperation. Love is the one thing that makes us all equally happy or miserable. It's very much like poverty—it doesn't discriminate either.

"Isn't it time for your break?" asks Jimena suddenly. I look at the clock on the register.

"You're right, it is."

I leave the store and find a quiet corner in the mall. I take a deep breath and pull my phone from my pocket.

I read Antero's text quickly.

I hug my phone and stare at the people who are talking and laughing all around me.

I feel as if my life just corrected itself.

It wasn't me or anything I did or didn't do.

Antero's text was brief and to the point. He explained he got cold feet at the thought of us moving together. He felt his whole life was planned for him by everyone else and he felt as if he was drowning. He wasn't ready to settle down yet. He wanted to live his life first. It didn't mean he didn't love me. In fact, he wanted to tell me all about it, but he was afraid I would have changed his mind because of how much he loved me. He realized later that he needed to explain, but by then he couldn't find me.

I wish Antero had told me two and a half years ago. But I understand also why he didn't. Love pulls us even when we know it's taking us to places where we don't want to go. I asked Greg to stay although I knew he was bad news. Love is just like life, it leads us down unknown paths and sometimes we have to change direction. I stare at my phone for a moment. I want to tell Antero I understand him more than he knows; that I respect his choice, but something in me resists the idea. Perhaps it's pride. He did leave me wondering for more than two years.

I type a brief message; I wish him all happiness in the future. I stare at the words for a full minute before I press send.

I feel strange. I'm about to get divorced and I just figured out what went wrong with Antero. I feel as if I just finished two books. Now I just need to find a new one to read.

My phone beeps.

It's Miguel. He's sent me a gif of falling hearts. I can feel a smile rise up to my eyes as I put my phone in my pocket.

I don't need to find another book.

I'm already reading a new one.

27

We walk slowly through the Millennium Park. I listen to Miguel as he talks about Chicago and its history. I could listen to his voice all day. It's soothing, but not in a sleep-inducing way. It's more like a soft summer breeze on the beach.

We cross the pedestrian bridge and pass the playground. I see people moving at a high speed in front of us. After a moment's confusion I realize they are skating. I can feel my eyes light up.

"Do you know how to skate?" I ask, turning to look at Miguel.

"Of course I do," laughs Miguel.

"Can we go?"

I feel like a little kid, but I don't care. It's been too long. I used to skate several times a week in Finland. Greg didn't ever want to go. He would play ice hockey with his friends, but he didn't ever want to skate with me. He said it was ridiculous to skate around in a circle.

"You want to go skating?" asks Miguel, turning to look at the ice skating ribbon.

"Yes!"

I see apprehension in Miguel's eyes.

"Never mind, it was a silly idea," I say and look away.

"Hey," he says, squeezing my hand. "We can go. I was

just thinking about when we have to be back. I promised *Abuela* I would take her shopping."

My smile returns. Miguel's kindness catches me still by surprise most days, but I'm slowly getting used to it.

I begin to walk quickly toward the entrance. I feel Miguel pulling me back gently.

"Hey, slow down!" he says laughing. "I don't want you to fall. There's ice on the ground and you don't have your skates on yet."

I stop and press my lips together to hide another smile. I don't know what I've done to deserve Miguel. He's not perfect, but he's perfect for me. He makes me feel beautiful and loved like no other man ever has. Just being with him has made my self-esteem rise like a phoenix from the ashes.

This is what love should feel like all the time.

I stop by the railing. I pull my mittens off, adjust my hat and wrap my scarf tighter around my neck. Miguel stops next to me.

"Where did you learn to skate like that?" he asks with admiration in his voice.

"On the ice like everyone else," I say, laughing.

"It must have been one hell of an ice."

"I've been skating since I was four. It's normal in Finland."

"Wow, well, I wish I was as good as you."

I put my mittens back on, give Miguel a kiss and skate

away. I turn and skate backwards. I smile and motion with my hands for Miguel to come and get me. Suddenly I see someone staring at me from a bench. I feel as if time stops and everything freezes around me. A split second later time begins to move again. I realize I'm still moving too. I turn my head to look at Miguel and lose my balance. I feel the cold ice underneath me as I slide toward the railing.

Miguel skates to me and gets on his knees next to me.

"Are you okay?"

"Yeah, I'm fine. I just… lost my balance. It's okay."

I get up and brush the snow off my legs.

I glance toward the bench.

Greg's gone.

28

I see Jimena running through the store. Even when she runs she looks gorgeous. A few weeks ago I would have been jealous. I *was* jealous, but Miguel has made me feel gorgeous too. I'm beginning to understand how Jimena feels most of the time. I can't blame her for feeling the way she does. It's a nice feeling. But something in me says there has to be more to life than just feeling pretty.

Jimena hugs me and causes me to nearly lose my balance.

"*¡Mi marido viene!*"

She pulls away and grabs my arms.

"He's coming, my husband is finally coming! I can't believe it! I get to finally see him again!" exclaims Jimena, laughing and crying at the same time.

"That's wonderful news, Jimena! When is he going to be here?"

"Sometime next month. He got the approval yesterday. He just needs to wrap up things in Mexico."

"I'm really happy for you," I say smiling again.

Jimena wipes her eyes.

"*¡Ay, Dios mio!* Did I smear my makeup? I have to go fix it. I'll be right back."

"But—"

"If you see the manager, just tell her I have women's issues."

I watch as Jimena walks quickly through the store. I glance around to see if the manager is anywhere nearby. I decide to forget about it. I don't think Jimena will get in trouble even if she's spotted. I bet even the manager has looked forward to this moment.

We all have.

I get off the bus and walk toward Miguel's apartment.

I open the front door and take off my jacket. Miguel comes from the kitchen and gives me a kiss.

"*Hola, mi amor,* how was your day?"

"It was good."

"Did Jimena tell you her news?"

"It was all she talked about!" I say laughing.

"It's great news, yes? As soon as Carlos is finally here Jimena will be too busy to run everyone else's lives. We all get a break."

I just smile. If it wasn't for Jimena, I wouldn't have left Greg and met Miguel. Her meddling isn't the worst thing that has ever happened to me.

"Hey, I was thinking we could get some take out and watch a movie. Sound good?"

"Yeah, sounds good."

"What do you want? Thai? Mexican? Puerto Rican?"

"Why don't you choose?"

Miguel gives me an amused smile.

"What?"

"You're becoming an American. You can't make up your mind."

"That's not true! I just don't know the restaurants in the area."

"Okay, fair enough," says Miguel, returning to the kitchen. I can tell the amused smile is still on his lips by the way he shakes his head. I feel my cheeks burn. I don't even know why I feel so offended. I guess it's the old dislike that hasn't left me entirely. I didn't like Americans before I came here and I certainly never thought I was going to set a foot in this country. I didn't like their arrogance then and I'm not so sure I like it any better now, but it's not as bad as I thought. I don't think there's anything wrong with people feeling confident; it only becomes a problem when it goes overboard. The same thing is true of shyness; there's nothing wrong with it, unless it prevents you from actually living.

I go to the living room and sit down on the couch. I turn on the TV and scroll through the movies.

"The food should be here in about twenty minutes. What do you want to watch?" asks Miguel, sitting down next to me. I'm about to shrug when I stop myself. Miguel is right, this isn't me. I need to learn to speak my mind again.

"Why don't we watch a thriller?"

"A thriller? Awesome!" Oh, by the way, do you want something to drink?"

"Yeah, sure. I'll have sparkling water, if you have some."

"I do actually," says Miguel and gets up.

I smile to myself. It's funny what love does to you.

I don't need to drink anymore.
Love is enough.

29

Miguel puts a dress on the counter and smiles at me.

"I hope you like it."

I give him a puzzled look.

"Jimena said you would."

I glance at Jimena who gives me one of her enigmatic smiles.

"Yeah, sure…" I say and blush mildly.

I scan the tag, fold the dress and put it in a bag. Miguel pays and takes the bag from me.

"I actually came to ask if you want to go dancing tonight."

"Dancing? Isn't it the middle of the week?"

"You can go dancing any day of the week," says Miguel with an amused smile.

"What kind of dancing?" I ask carefully.

"Have you ever tried salsa?"

I bite my lower lip. I'm not a good dancer and I don't think I can do salsa, but the look on Miguel's face is so eager I can't say no.

"I haven't, but I guess I can try it?"

"Great! I'll pick you up around seven?"

"Ok."

I watch as Miguel leaves the store. I turn to look at Jimena.

"I think I need your help."

"Oh? What do you need?" asks Jimena, glancing at me.

"What do people wear when they go salsa dancing?"

"A tight dress and high heels."

"Of course…."

Jimena puts the hangers in the bin and turns to look at me.

"When is your shift over?"

"Four."

"Perfect! Come by my place after work. I have what you need.'"

"Thanks."

I stare at the register for a moment. I know Jimena means well, and I'm thankful, but if New Year's Eve was any indication I know exactly what kind of dress I can look forward to—one that leaves nothing to the imagination.

I look out the window. Miguel sent me a text twenty minutes ago to let me know he was on his way. I glance at the sky. The heavy snowfall shows no sign of letting up. It will be a miracle if he makes it in this weather.

I'm about to turn around when I notice a figure by the streetlight on the other side of the street. It's standing in the shadow, but I can tell it's looking in my direction.

Miguel parks his car in front of the gate. I wave at him to let him know I'm coming.

The figure turns and begins to walk away.

I'd recognize that walk from anywhere.

It's Greg.

It's the second time I've seen him watching me. I glance at Miguel. My skin feels suddenly cold and sweaty at the same time. I realize Greg's seen Miguel. And not just seen him; he's seen him with me.

Greg always said he would kill anyone who came near me and that he would make me pay too. I wasn't sure if he meant it literally, but the look on his face told me it wasn't exactly a joke. We don't live together anymore, but we're still married. I'm sure he still sees me as his wife and that means he thinks he owns me. I wonder if I should tell Miguel about it, but I don't want to worry him unnecessarily. Maybe I should talk to Jimena first. She knows American men much better than I do. I'm sure she'll have something wise to say.

I grab my keys and lock the door behind me.

The club is packed. Miguel was right. People do dance every night of the week here.

I wait for Miguel to order us drinks. A man slides next to me.

"*¡Que linda!* Very pretty!" he says while he eyes me from head to toe.

"And *very* taken," says Miguel and gives the man a look that tells him to move on.

"Sorry bro, didn't see you there."

I watch as the man moves to the next woman. He repeats the same line. I wonder if it has ever worked. The woman follows him to the dance floor. I guess it has and does.

"Miguel?"

I turn my head. I see a young woman standing next to Miguel. Her curly hair reaches halfway down her back and she's wearing the shortest skirt in the club.

"Oh, hi Katie, how are you?" says Miguel and gives her a quick side hug.

"I'm good. Um, I haven't seen you for a while, did you stop dancing?" asks Katie with a nervous smile.

"No, I've just been busy."

Katie glances at the people who are dancing. She bites her lower lip.

"Um… aren't you going to ask me to dance?"

"Oh, I'm sorry, this is Marja."

Katie turns to look at me. I can tell she's struggling to maintain her smile.

"Nice to meet you."

Her voice has a cold undertone only I can detect. I give her a brief smile.

"Okay, well, maybe later?"

"Yeah, sure," says Miguel and smiles.

I watch as Katie walks through the crowd toward the other side of the room. She turns her head a couple of times and looks at Miguel.

"Who was that?"

"Oh, Katie? She's just someone I've danced with a few times."

His eyes are evasive. I can tell he's done more than just dance with her. Miguel notices the look in my eyes. He grabs me by my waist and pulls me closer.

"You have nothing to worry about. I have only eyes for you," he says and gives me a kiss. "Come, let's dance."

I follow him to the dance floor, my heart filled with trepidation. He takes my right hand and places his right hand on my waist.

"Just relax, you'll do great."

I take off my shoes and fall on the couch. My feet hurt, but it was worth it. I haven't had that much fun in a long time.

"Tired?" asks Miguel, standing by the doorway.

"A bit," I say laughing. "I didn't know salsa could be that much fun."

"Well, you're fun to be with *and* you're a natural. I've never seen anyone learn to dance that fast."

I glance at Miguel and try not to smile. No one has ever said I'm fun to be with, but then again I've never spent time with someone like Miguel before. He has the ability to bring all kinds of hidden aspects to the surface I didn't even know existed in me. I lean forward and stretch my back. As I suspected, the dress Jimena had waiting for me was tighter than Saran Wrap. I tried to say I didn't want to wear it, but Jimena just rolled her eyes and said a man wants to see a woman's body.

"Can I borrow some clothes from you? I want to get out

of this thing."

"Yeah, sure, help yourself. I'll go take a shower."

I go to the bedroom and grab the same sweater I've worn before. I find a pair of pajama pants and put them on. I know I look positively unsexy, but I don't care. I've looked sexy long enough today. All the eyes that rested on my body all night made me feel like I was on display again. I know some women enjoy it, but I've never been one of them.

I return to the living room and sit down on the couch. Miguel comes from the bathroom a few minutes later. A scent lingers around him as if he has just come from the forest where pine, cedar and earth mix together. He sits down next to me on the couch. He rubs his neck with his left hand and looks away for a moment. I give him a look that asks what's going on. He glances at me a couple of times and looks at his hands.

"I… have something I… need to talk to you about."

I look at him. He looks nervous and serious at the same time.

"I'm sure Jimena has told you I've never had a serious girlfriend."

"She did," I say carefully.

"It's not that I haven't wanted one, it's just that I've never met a woman I've wanted to be with for more than a few weeks."

I look at Miguel with a confused look. Suddenly I realize what he's getting at.

Shit!

He's breaking up with me!

I look away. I'm sure this has to do with the Katie person we met tonight. Maybe he realized he wants to be with her instead of me. I close my eyes briefly. I don't even know why I'm upset. I knew this moment was coming, but I guess I just assumed we were going to have this conversation just before I was leaving.

I turn to face Miguel and give him a look that asks him to please just say it. He looks at me and for a moment he looks confused as if his train of thought has been interrupted.

"I, um... I know we've only been going out for a month and I know you're still married, but I just..."

Miguel shakes his head and looks away again. I can hear him mutter something in Spanish. He turns to look at me again. I see something nakedly vulnerable in his eyes.

"I know I shouldn't even be asking this, but I would like you to be my girlfriend, the serious kind, the kind that leads to something more than just dating."

I can feel the whole room begin to spin. I try to steady my breathing. I know Miguel thinks I'm shocked because we're moving too fast. How am I supposed to tell him I have to return to Finland? That I never thought he was going to be serious about me in the first place?

I feel Miguel looking at me. I turn to look at him.

"Just think about it, ok?"

"I will," I say and force a smile.

Miguel's expression relaxes. He asks if I'm thirsty. I nod and watch as he goes to the kitchen.

I stare into nothingness.

I've finally met the man of my dreams and now I'm going to have to say goodbye to him.

But what's new?

This is how it always ends.

30

I pace the floor with my phone in my hand.

Miguel called a few minutes ago and asked if I wanted to go out to dinner. I told him I was doing laundry. It wasn't exactly a lie, but I could have done the laundry and still had time to meet him. I know I can't see him; not before I have an answer to give him. I have to think about it, although I know there's nothing to think about. I have to tell him the truth. And I want to, but the truth sounds too cruel even for me.

I turn to look at my cat on the couch. It looks at me as if wanting to know what the fuss is all about.

"*Olisi kiva jos voisit auttaa.* But of course you can't help me. No one can."

I close my eyes briefly. I know I'm not upset just because I have to say goodbye to Miguel. I was beginning to like my life here in this city although it's still loud and drives me crazy most of the time. I was finally beginning to shed the seriousness that always prevented me from enjoying my life. I know I can be someone here that I can't at home. But it's all over now. I have to say goodbye to Chicago too.

I stare at my phone. Maybe I should call Miguel back and just get it over with. I take a deep breath. I find his number from the contact list and press the green call button.

I hit the red circle a split second later.

I close my eyes again.

I can't tell him over the phone.

I throw my phone on the table, sit down on the couch and cover my face with my hands. Leaving Greg was a walk in the park compared to this. I feel like such an idiot. I know I've been acting as if all of this was going to last forever. I should have told Miguel the truth in the beginning. I should have been honest. But something in me didn't want to be honest. I wanted to be with him so desperately that I denied reality.

And here we are.

A lonely tear finds its way down my cheek. I know I have only myself to blame for this whole mess. I knew I would fall in love, I always do, and I don't mind that my heart is going to break again, but how could I have done this to Miguel? He's been nothing but nice to me, loved me like no one else ever has, and now I'm going to break his heart too. I'm sure he'll never want to see me again.

I wouldn't want to.

My cat pushes its head against my arm. I stroke its back and get a pleased purr as a response. I watch as my cat closes its eyes slowly. I'm going to have to say goodbye to my cat too, my only friend who has been with me through all of it. I grab my cat and hug it. It stays still for once and looks at me with its serious eyes. Maybe it knows why I'm upset. Maybe it doesn't want me to leave either.

"*Mä haluan jäädä tänne,*" I whisper into my cat's fur.

But I know I can't stay. I would have to stay married to Greg until we can file for the removal of conditions and we would have to live together to make our marriage real enough for the immigration officials. I doubt they approve of marriages where the couple doesn't live together. The whole idea makes me shiver. After feeling Miguel's gentle and caring touch, the thought of Greg touching me repulses me. His touch was harsh and void of feeling most of the time. All he cared about was his own pleasure. I'd rather die than go back to living with him. But if I don't, I can't have a life with Miguel.

It's Sophie's choice. There are no happy endings here.

I can feel my cat begin to wriggle. I relax my hold and let it jump back on the couch. My cat gives me an annoyed look and begins to lick itself. Cats know how to soothe themselves. I wish I had a bottle of wine to soothe myself too, but I haven't bought any in more than two weeks. Besides I know if I drink I'm going to call Miguel and who knows what I will say.

I stare at the wall for a moment. I know I can go home and hope Miguel will want to file a fiancé visa application to bring me here, but we've known each other for less than two months. Do I really want to take that risk again? What if he'll change too and I'll end up here—again—just waiting to go home? Miguel's never had a serious girlfriend. What if he can't handle having one? What if he is just being sentimental right now and he'll change his mind when things get really serious—marriage kind of serious. Besides, I don't want my future to be in the hands of a man. I don't want to live my life that way. I want to be in charge of my own life. I want to make my own decisions and I want the freedom to leave if I want without coercion and the endless bureaucratic nightmare that comes from being in a strange country with a conditional residency.

"So, that's it," I say to the wall and get up.

I'm about to go back to the laundry room when my phone rings.

31

I unlock the door.

I hear soft music. I close the door and take my jacket and shoes off. I go to the living room and look around. I see a blanket on the floor. Candles are burning on the table and on the shelves. I see petals on the floor and a bouquet on the table.

I can feel someone standing behind me. I turn around.

"Happy Valentine's Day, *mi amor,*" says Miguel softly and kisses me. I look at him for a moment and bite my lower lip. I wish I had remembered it was Valentine's Day. It's not something Finns celebrate as a couple; it's a friendship day in Finland. I know I look terrible. My hair is wet from the soggy rain and my makeup disappeared hours ago. I wish I could take a shower and make myself more presentable.

"You're always beautiful," says Miguel as if he's read my mind. "Besides, we can take a shower later."

I see the mischievous look in his eyes. Jimena has the same look when she talks about sex.

I sit down on the blanket. Miguel opens a bottle of sparkling wine. He fills one of the glasses and hands it to me. He fills another glass for himself and sits down next to me.

"So, what should we toast to?"

"I don't know," I say and laugh mildly.

"How about to a beautiful year together."

"A year? We've only been together for six weeks."

"I was talking about the year ahead of us."

I take a sip of the wine to hide my smile. I see tenderness and something deeper in Miguel's eyes. It's as if he has finally been given the gift he has waited for all of his life.

"*Mi novia…*" he whispers and caresses my cheek.

I know what the words mean now. He used them last Friday when I said I wanted to be his girlfriend more than anything in the world. He smiled and whispered the words just before he kissed me like I've never been kissed before. His kiss was passionate, tender, and hungry all in one. I lost myself in his kiss and I thanked God and all the angels in heaven there is a way for me to stay.

. . . .

Sara called last Thursday. She told me she had a feeling she needed to talk to me. I broke down into tears and told her everything from the beginning, how Greg had left me and gone back to his ex-wife, how I had been all by myself and how I had met Miguel and I didn't know if I wanted to return to Finland. She listened without interrupting. In the end she told me to check my email in a few minutes. Samuli was going to send me a few links. After we hung up I looked up the sites. They were filled with information how I could apply for permanent residency on my own without Greg. There were a lot of things I would have to prove, but at least I had a chance to stay.

. . . . . **. . . . .**

"What's wrong?" asks Miguel with concern in his voice.

I give him a confused look. A split second later I realize I must have disappeared into my own thoughts.

"Oh, um… nothing… I just realized I didn't get you anything."

Miguel smiles at me.

"You're here, aren't you?"

He takes my glass and puts it on the table. I smile at him as he leans me down on the blanket and kisses me.

32

Miguel opens the door for me. I can hear music and excited chatter coming from the living room. The apartment is packed with people; everyone has come to get a glimpse of Carlos. He arrived a week ago, but no one has seen him yet. I can't fault Jimena for wanting to keep her husband to herself the first few days. Waiting for nearly two years must have felt like an eternity.

"Marja!" calls Jimena from the other end of the living room. She walks quickly to me and takes my hand.

"Come! I want you to meet my husband."

She drags me through the crowd.

"Carlos, this is Marja, *mi amiga.*"

Carlos gets up and kisses me on the cheek.

"¡*Hola,* Marja, *mucho gusto*!"

I stare at him unable to speak. He is even more handsome in real life than in photos; he looks just like a movie star. The situation reminds me of the time I met Miguel for the first time. I tried to say something then too, but the words just didn't come out.

"¡*Hola,* Carlos! Glad you're finally here! Jimena has been waiting for you for a long time."

"*Si,* we've waited much time," says Carlos and shakes Miguel's hand.

I watch as Jimena sits down on Carlos' lap. She caresses

his hair and looks at him with eyes filled with pure love and wonder, as if she can't believe he's finally here.

Miguel gives me a look and pulls me aside.

"Let's leave the lovebirds alone," he says, laughing.

I follow him to the kitchen and sit down by the table. It seems to be Miguel's favorite room in every house we go to. I'm not sure if it's because the food is there or because it's quiet. He enjoys partying just as much as everyone else in his family, but he seems to always seek out a quiet space whenever we go out.

I watch as *Abuela* Rosalita rinses a plate and puts it away. She addresses Miguel who smiles and responds in Spanish. I give him a look that asks what they are talking about.

"*Abuela* asked if you're my *novia* from Finland. I said yes, you're my girlfriend and that I love you very much."

I feel my cheeks flush. *Abuela* Rosalita looks at me and smiles. Her eyes are kind. I can tell now where Miguel gets his kindness from. I listen as she continues to talk. I look at Miguel waiting for him to translate.

"*Abuela* says she knows what you're going through. She came here as an immigrant too and she knows it's hard, but it's worth it because of the people who love you, because they are your real home. As long as you're with people who love you, you're home."

"That's beautiful," I say with a voice barely louder than a whisper.

A sudden commotion startles us. Miguel gets up. I look at him, unsure if I should go with him. He motions with his hand for me to stay.

Abuela Rosalita wipes her hands on a towel and sits down next to me.

"Miguel is a good boy. *Siempre te va a amar*, he will love you, always," she says and pats my hand.

I want to say something, but the words get stuck again. All I can do is nod and smile.

Miguel returns and looks at both of us. He says something in Spanish to his grandmother who just smiles and gets up. He looks at me. His eyes ask what is going on. I shrug. What is said between women doesn't need to be repeated to men. That's at least what Jimena says. At this moment I agree with her.

"O-*kay*…. Hey, everyone's going out. Do you want to go?"

"Sure," I say and turn to smile at Miguel's grandmother.

We share a look.

We don't speak the same language, but we don't need to.

We know what the other thinks.

I stand by the bar and sip my drink. Isabella slides next to me and orders tequila shots. She turns to look at me and crosses her arms.

"So, you finally tamed our Miguel, huh? It was about time. We thought he'd never find a woman who was able to put up with him."

"Hey, Isabella! I don't see a ring on your finger," says Miguel with a wry smile.

"So? I'm four years younger than you are, I've got time."

"Yeah? You keep on telling yourself that. Maybe one day one of your many boyfriends will come back."

"Hey, Miguel, bite me!" says Isabella grabbing the shot glasses from the counter.

Miguel laughs and shakes his head.

I watch as Isabella returns to the small group that stands by a table near the dancefloor.

"I don't think she likes me," I say, glancing at Isabella again.

"Don't worry about Isabella, that's just how she is. Everyone loves you, *abuela* especially. She said she could tell you're a good woman and that you will make me very happy. I agreed with her," says Miguel with a warm smile.

I glance at him. I guess they had that conversation while I was talking to Jimena who was fussing about the length of my skirt; it wasn't short enough in her opinion. I know I shouldn't worry, but I can't help but feel insecure. Greg's family kept on talking about Alene as if Greg was still married to her even after he married me. I barely saw any of them during the time we lived together.

I can feel Miguel looking at me. He puts his right hand under my chin. I know what that means; he's seeking eye contact. I turn my head and look him in the eyes.

"Hey, you have nothing to worry about. If anyone in my family gives you any grief, you just let me know, okay?" he says and pulls me close to himself. "I want you to be happy."

I lean my head against Miguel's chest and watch as

Jimena and Carlos slow dance to a fast song. I feel a smile appear on my lips. A few months ago both Jimena and I were brokenhearted for different reasons. Now we're both happy for the same reason.

Sometimes life surprises us with happiness when we least expect it.

33

I get off the bus and wait for Miguel who is helping an elderly woman with her shopping cart. Chicago is still a mess of melting snow and trash, but I barely notice it. It's as if love has filled my veins with warm air. I feel as if I'm floating most of the time. I know the feeling will end soon, but for now I'm enjoying it.

We walk toward the movie theater. I look at the posters as we pass them. Miguel tells me I should be in a movie too. I tell him he should stop being silly and give him a kiss as he opens the door for me.

I have barely entered the building when I see Greg walking toward us.

"Maria! Nice to see you."

I feel my whole body freeze.

I stare at Greg who has a smirk on his face. I don't like the way he smiles. He gives Miguel a once-over.

"Oh, so you're the guy who is fucking my wife."

Greg tilts his head and looks at me.

"Is this why you asked me to leave? So you could be with this clown?"

"Aren't you with Alene?" I ask with a cold voice.

Greg laughs.

"We're just friends! How many times do I have to explain it to you? I thought your English would have improved by now."

I look away.

"But I guess I should file for a divorce since you don't seem to know what marriage means."

"Please do," I say with a defiance that surprises even me.

Greg looks at me through narrowed eyes; I can see something dark in them. He turns to look at Miguel.

"I wouldn't waste my time on this one if I were you."

He brushes against my body as he passes me. I close my eyes. I feel cold all over as if I've been plunged into a river in the middle of winter; as if all happiness has been sucked out of me and I'm back in the darkness.

"Are you okay?" asks Miguel, placing his hand on my shoulder.

"Yeah, just... give me a minute."

I take several deep breaths. Slowly the shock begins to subside. I glance at Miguel. He's staring at Greg through the large windows. I can tell he's struggling to remain calm.

I watch as Greg reaches the crosswalk. He turns to look at me just as the light turns green.

He shakes his head slowly.

I know what that means.

He's telling me I'm going to regret this.

I take a quick shower. I rush back to the bedroom and put on clean jeans and a clean sweater. I glance at my phone. The bus is going to be here in less than ten minutes.

I find my cat and hug it.

"I'm so sorry I have to leave you again, but Miguel is waiting for me. I'll see you tomorrow, ok?"

I give my cat a kiss and put it back down on the floor. I walk to the front door. I'm about to put my shoes on when I see the doorknob turning.

I hear a soft knock.

"Maria, open the door, I know you're home."

I stare at the door.

It's Greg.

I know he has a key, but the door has a deadbolt—he can't get in.

"Come on Maria, open the door. I just want to talk to you."

I know he doesn't want to just talk; he never did. A dark, sticky feeling fills me. He's never hit me, but the look in his eyes earlier today told me he was considering it. I know he'll force himself on me, he always did when he was mad at me, but I don't know if I'm going to end up in the hospital or if he'll kill me. I'm beginning to think he's capable of it.

I retreat to the living room and look around frantically. I need to get out of this apartment, but how? I think about using the backdoor, but I know he'll catch me if I do. My cat meows every time I leave. He'll hear it. I can't leave without him finding out.

"Maria! Open the door!"

I turn and stare at the door. I can tell his voice is getting angrier. I can feel panic growing in me. I know the door won't keep him out for long.

"Open the door!! Did you hear me!?"

I pull my phone from my pocket and dial Miguel's number.

"Come on, come on, answer!" I plead, while the pounding increases.

The ringing ends. I hear a voice tell me the number I've dialed is not available at the moment. I leave a quick message and hang up. I retreat to the couch and stare at the door. I can feel my breathing become shallow.

"Goddammit Maria, I'm still your husband! Open this door, *now!*" yells Greg, kicking the door. "*Open* the *door!* I swear I'm going to break this damn thing if you don't open this door *right now!*"

I hear a loud crack as the door frame begins to give way. I begin to dial 911 with shaky hands. Suddenly I see blue flashing lights appear on the walls. I walk quickly to the window and look out. I see two police cars parked outside. I watch as four police officers get out of the cars and stand by the metal gate. It's locked, they can't get in.

The pounding stops.

I watch as Greg leaves the building and opens the gate.

He talks to the officers.

I see one of them nodding.

"Don't listen to him," I whisper as tears fill my eyes.

I watch as two of the officers begin to get ready to leave. I slide down to the floor and stare at the empty TV-table as tears fill my eyes again. I know he's told them a story that makes him the victim. Somehow all of this is my fault. The police are going to leave and Greg will come up here. He'll break the door and he'll break me too. I cover my face with my hands. I never thought my life was going to end this way. I came here to live and now I'm going to die.

I hear someone knocking on the door.

"Police! Open the door!"

I wipe my eyes, get up and walk quickly to the front door. I unlock the deadbolt and open the door.

"We got a call about a domestic disturbance."

I look at the officers. I try to say something, but English seems to have escaped me.

"Is the man outside your husband?"

I look at the officer. She looks almost like one of my aunts. It's enough to get my mind working again.

"He is, but… he doesn't live here anymore."

"He doesn't live here with you?"

"No, he left. He's filing for a divorce."

The officer who has done all the talking looks at the other officer. They share a look.

"Do you have somewhere safe to go tonight?"

"I—"

Tears flood my eyes again. I try to stop them, but I can't. How can I explain I have nowhere to go? I can't afford a hotel, Jimena is out with Carlos, and Miguel doesn't answer his phone. I don't know anyone else.

One of the other officers enters the building and motions for the talking officer to come outside. I stand by the door inside my apartment and stare at the dirty welcome mat outside the door. I feel numb. I know Greg is just waiting

216

for the police to leave and I'm just waiting for the inevitable. I know the police can't protect me. No one can.

The talking officer returns.

"There's someone outside who says he's your friend. Do you want to talk to him?"

I give the officer a confused look.

"Do you want him to come up here?"

I wipe my eyes and try to think.

"Um… sure…"

I don't know why I said that. I don't know who it could be. Suddenly the thought comes to me. Maybe it's one of Greg's friends. Maybe they'll take turns. The thought makes me want to vomit.

The officer who hasn't spoken yet goes outside. A moment later I see Carlos by the gate. He walks to me and asks if I'm okay. I nod. I don't understand why he's here.

"Miguel is coming, Jimena is outside."

A minute later I see Miguel running up the stairs. He runs to me and envelops me in his arms. I can hear his labored breathing; I know it's not just from the running.

"Oh God, Marja… I didn't hear my phone—"

He pulls away abruptly and cups my face with his hands. He looks at me with searching eyes.

"He didn't hurt you, did he?"

I shake my head. Suddenly everything around me begins to spin. It's as if the hallway is expanding and contracting at the same time. I feel as if I'm slipping into another realm.

"Marja? *Marja!*"

I can hear Miguel's voice as from far away.

I wake up.

Miguel is on his knees next to me. I look around. Why am I on the floor?

"What happened?" I ask with a weak voice.

"You fainted. Can you get up?"

"I think so."

Miguel takes my hand and helps me up to my feet. The officer who has done all the talking tilts her head.

"Do you need us to call an ambulance?"

"No, I'm fine."

The officer talks into the radio and turns to address Miguel.

"It would be best if she didn't spend the night here."

"I agree. I'll take her home with me."

"You have five minutes to pack. We'll wait outside."

Miguel turns to look at me.

"Just take what you need for tonight. We can come later to get the rest."

I nod and walk to the bedroom. I pull my bag from the shelf and throw random clothes in it. I go to the kitchen to get a plastic bag. I sweep all the things from the bathroom shelf right into it.

I return to the living room.

My cat!

"What are you looking for?" asks Miguel.

"My cat! I can't leave it here."

Miguel looks under the couch.

"I think it's here."

He lifts the couch and waits for me to pull my cat to

myself. It doesn't resist. I suspect it understands what is going on. I go back to the bedroom and pull the carrier from the closet. I put my cat in it. It gives me an annoyed look as I close the zipper. It's the only semblance of normalcy I've seen all night.

"Do you need anything else?"

I shake my head.

Miguel picks my bag from the floor and goes to the hallway. I lock the door to the apartment and walk to the gate after Miguel. I see Greg standing by one of the police cars. His eyes are dark from rage. He knows his lies didn't work this time.

Miguel guides me to walk to the left.

"I think that cat belongs to me," calls Greg after me.

I ignore him and keep on walking.

I see Jimena and a few other people next to Miguel's car. Jimena is wearing a long red dress. She looks as if she's on her way to a party.

Jimena rushes to me and puts her hands on my shoulders.

"Oh my God, Marja! Are you okay?"

"I'm fine," I say with a weak voice.

Jimena gives Miguel a look. I can tell she's not.

"Uncle Tino and Pablo are here. I called them."

"I don't think that would help right now."

"We can't let that bastard get away with it!" exclaims Jimena, her eyes blazing.

"I think we should just let it be for now."

"And what if he comes back for her again?"

"Then he gets to deal with me!"

I can hear the tension in Miguel's voice. Jimena looks away and shakes her head.

"We'll talk about it later, okay?" says Miguel and opens the passenger side door. He helps me into the car and closes the door.

I hold my cat in its carrier and stare at the building that has been my home for almost eighteen months.

I have a feeling I will never see it again.

34

I close the bathroom door and return to the living room.

I lie back down on the couch and rest my head on Miguel's lap. He caresses my hair and glances at me every few seconds as if wanting to make sure I'm still there. He hasn't let me out of his sight ever since Greg tried to break into my apartment. He even changed his work schedule to be able to take me to work and pick me up. I tried to tell him he didn't have to, but he just shook his head and said there was nothing to discuss. Jimena told me it was the least he could do when I asked her why he insisted. She said if he had been smart he would have let Uncle Tino and Pablo deal with the situation. That way there wouldn't be a situation to deal with now. I had no idea what she meant and I didn't ask.

I stare at the TV without seeing the image. I've been trying to forget what happened, but my mind just doesn't seem to let me. At work I think I see Greg standing in the crowd, smiling at me. I can feel him following me when I walk to the restroom. He taunts me and tells me he can always come back and finish what he started.

He's everywhere and yet nowhere.

Just like he was that night.

· · · · · • · · · · ·

I remember arriving at Miguel's apartment with my cat. I put the carrier on the floor and for a moment I just stood there in the middle of the living room wondering if I was dreaming; if I was still in my apartment waiting for the door to break or if I was already dead. I ran to the bathroom and vomited until there was nothing left in me. I sat down on the bathroom floor and cried hysterically. Miguel lifted me up and carried me to bed.

I remember lying in bed, drifting in and out all night. In my dreams Greg broke the door and sent me flying across the room. He ripped my shirt off and laughed at me as I tried to cover myself. He forced himself on me and beat me until I could taste the blood, until he had broken every bone in my body and there was nothing left to break. I woke up several times crying, begging him to stop. Miguel held me tighter each time until I drifted back to sleep.

. . . . . ＿＿ . . . . .

My phone beeps.

I sit up and look at the text. I feel sick to my stomach when I see who it's from.

"What is it?" asks Miguel, seeing the look on my face.

I hand my phone to him.

"Yeah, no, you're not meeting him."

"But I need to get the divorce papers somehow. I don't want to give him your address. I don't want him to know where I am!"

Miguel exhales and rubs his forehead with his left hand.

"Okay, fine. Tell him we'll meet him in front of the courthouse in two hours."

"Why there?"

"There are always plenty of police around."

I see something hard in his eyes. I get the feeling the police aren't going to be there to protect me from Greg.

I look around.

Greg is late.

I know he's doing it on purpose. He doesn't like to be told what to do. He tried to argue about the location, but Miguel took my phone and told him if he didn't like it, we could meet at the police station where they already knew him. He didn't argue after that.

I spot him finally by the traffic lights. He smiles as he walks toward us. I can see contempt in his eyes, the kind that always sent cold chills down my spine. He stops a couple of steps away from us.

"I see you brought your lover-boy with you."

"Just give her the papers," counters Miguel.

Greg gives him a vicious look.

"We wouldn't be here if you had kept your hands off my wife so why don't you just shut up!"

I glance at Miguel. I can see his hands forming into fists.

"Please, just give them to me," I say, trying to hide the fact that my knees are about to give way at any moment.

"Sure," says Greg, smiling again. He takes a step closer

and hands me the envelope. I try to take it from him, but he doesn't let go.

Our eyes meet.

He has the same look in his eyes he had when he wanted to let me know I had done something unforgivable and that I would pay—one way or the other.

Miguel takes a step forward. Greg glances at him. I can tell he wishes we weren't in public from the murderous look in his eyes. Suddenly his expression relaxes. He let's go of the envelope and takes a step back. He looks away for a moment. When he looks at me again the smile has returned.

"The owner wants eight hundred for the doorframe. You should pay, don't you think?"

I stare at Greg in disbelief.

"I mean, if it wasn't for you, the door would never have been damaged. You should have just opened it like I asked."

I recognize the threatening undertone in his voice. I know it's not about money; he has plenty. He just wants to punish me because I didn't do what he told me to.

"Come on, let's go," says Miguel quietly. He places his hand on my back and turns me to the right. I wonder why at first, but then I realize he placed himself between Greg and myself. He's not taking any chances.

I can feel Greg staring at us as we walk toward Miguel's car.

"Hey, pal! Are you sure you want this one? As far as I can tell she's already slept with half of Chicago!"

I can hear him spitting on the ground.

"Just keep walking," says Miguel with a tense voice.

Miguel opens the car door for me. I get in and hug the envelope. I feel nauseous. I don't think I will ever be able to see Greg or even think about him without wanting to vomit. Miguel gets in the car and glances at Greg who is still standing by the entrance. He shakes his head as he turns on the engine.

"Jimena was right, I should have let Uncle Tino and Pablo beat the shit out of him."

35

"Are you sure you'll be okay?" asks Jimena.

"Of course I will! Miguel is going to be here in two minutes."

"No, I'll wait."

"Jimena! Carlos is waiting for you! I'll be fine for two minutes! There are about a million people here!"

Jimena looks around. I've never seen her this serious.

"You have your phone, right?"

"I do."

"Okay, call Miguel if you see your ex. He knows to answer his phone this time."

"I will," I say and smile.

I watch as Jimena leaves reluctantly. I can tell she hasn't forgiven Miguel for his failure to answer when I called. I felt my face drain of all color when she told me if he had called her three minutes later, they would have been on the freeway and it would have been too late to turn around. If Carlos hadn't shown up when he did, who knows what would have happened? Maybe the police would have left and then what? How would Miguel been able to get to my apartment with the gate being locked? I know Miguel hasn't forgiven himself either. I tried to tell him it wasn't his fault, but he just shook his head and told me he should have answered the phone.

I see Miguel enter the building. He walks to me and looks around.

"Where's Jimena?"

"Carlos was waiting for her. I told her to go."

"And she left!?" exclaims Miguel, his eyes wide from shock and disbelief.

"It's okay, honestly."

Miguel sweeps the area with his eyes.

"Let's go," he says, glancing over his shoulder as he wraps his arm around my waist.

I scroll through the movies. I can feel a vague sense of boredom invade my mind. We haven't gone anywhere for more than a week. Miguel told me yesterday he didn't want me to work anymore. I told him I felt safer among other people. It wasn't exactly true, but true enough. I would go crazy being home all day by myself.

Miguel comes from the bathroom. He's changed into a clean T-shirt and sweatpants; his hair is still wet from the shower.

"Are you hungry? I can order a pizza."

"Sure."

Miguel goes to the kitchen and returns a few minutes later. He sits down next to me on the couch and pulls me to himself. I can feel the tension in his body. He hasn't been able to relax since that awful night and he seems to have an obsessive need to be near me at all times, as if he can't be sure I'm safe unless he can touch me at all times. I don't know how to help him. I want to tell him he doesn't have to protect me every minute of the day. But at the same time I want him to. I'm scared of Greg. I don't know what he'll do next, but I'm sure he'll try something. He's not the kind of a man to leave a job undone—other than our marriage, but I don't think he was ever committed to it in the first place. He was never there mentally even when he was there physically. I always felt I was alone, even when he was right next to me. It was as if I was literally invisible to him. We couldn't ever feel each other and of course we couldn't. How can you possibly feel someone who thinks of someone else all the time, who makes you feel he wishes you weren't there?

I know Miguel loves me and wants to be with me. He's always affirming his love for me as if he's convinced I will forget if he doesn't remind me. The difference is so stark I sometimes wonder why I didn't just leave Greg and go back home. But I know why. I wanted our relationship to work. Love makes us do things we wouldn't otherwise even when we lose ourselves in the process. Miguel has helped me find myself again, just as he has helped me find a whole new side of myself. It's as if two streams are filling a pool that has been left empty for too long. But underneath all of it, a constant anxiety keeps on churning, making my emotions feel stiff as butter. I wish I could end the anxiety, but to do so I would have to do something about Greg and it's a problem without a solution.

36

I watch as the wind throws the falling snow in every direction outside the mall. Miguel called me earlier and said he had to work longer than expected. Jimena told him she would keep me company. I would rather just go home than go out for dinner, but I know there is no arguing with Jimena.

I glance at my phone and wonder what's taking her so long. She went to the restroom to change into the new skirt she bought during her break.

That was twenty minutes ago.

I stare at the snow again. I know Greg is dangerous, but I don't know how long I'm going to be able to deal with this feeling I'm a witness who has to be escorted from one location to another to keep me safe. I had no freedom while I was with Greg and I feel he's still holding me captive although he's nowhere in sight.

I turn just in time to see Jimena coming down the escalator. She's wearing a grey coat and her boots reach to her knees. I always feel like I'm watching a fashion show when I see her.

"So, what do you think? It's divine, yes?" says Jimena, twirling to showcase her new skirt. I tell her she looks beautiful. She smiles and puts her white hat over her hair. She grabs my arm and tells me about the splendid time we'll have together.

The snow assaults my face the moment I open the door. I pull my hood up and try not to look straight ahead. We half-run down the nearly deserted street until we reach the restaurant.

We enter the small space. It's just as quiet as the street outside. We order our food and sit down by the window.

"So, three weeks till freedom! It must be a nice feeling," says Jimena and smiles.

"It is. I mean, I don't know if divorce is something anyone should celebrate," I say and try to smile.

"¡Ay, Marja! In your case, yes! You're allowed to celebrate! Your ex is a *complete* jerk, the sooner you're free, the better."

"I guess you're right," I say and take a sip of my drink.

Jimena looks at me.

"Are you still worried he'll come back?"

I glance at Jimena.

"I don't know.... I mean, I don't think he cares that much. I'm sure he's going to leave me alone after we get divorced."

Jimena presses her lips together and looks out the window. I can see her eyes narrow.

"Oh, well that's good!" she says and turns to look at me with enthusiasm.

I glance at Jimena. Why is she suddenly so enthusiastic? A moment ago she was concerned and suddenly she's pleased I'm not worried? I look out the window. I can only see more snow falling from the sky. I give Jimena another glance and decide to forget about it.

I pull the string and get up.

"Are you *sure* you don't want me to walk with you?" asks Jimena again.

"Yes, I'm sure! It's only one block," I say with a dismissive laugh. "What could happen?"

Jimena gives me another look, but doesn't say anything.

I get off the bus and begin to walk toward Miguel's apartment. The wind whips my face. I pull my hood up and turn my face away from the biting wind. I can feel the cold dig into my bones. The cold reminds me of my life with Greg. It left me feeling cold in every way. Good days were there for pretending; bad days were there for placating. But why do I keep on thinking about him? I haven't seen him since the day he gave me the divorce papers and I doubt I'll see him before our court date. I know he thinks he's sending me back home with the divorce. I'm sure it'll keep him happy.

I've almost reached the gate when I feel an arm wrap around my waist while another arm reaches across my body to my left shoulder.

I freeze.

I can hear heavy breathing next to my right ear.

"Did you really think I would let you make a fool out of me with your lover-boy?" says Greg in a low voice. "It's time you learned a lesson. You're coming with me!"

I can feel him beginning to drag me toward his car. It's enough to get me moving again.

"No!! Let me go!!" I scream. I grab his arm and try to pull it off, but he's too strong for me. The snow whirls around me. I can feel it on my face. It gets in my mouth and inside my jacket.

I can hear him opening a car door.

Panic takes over.

I kick the snow and try to remove his arm again.

"Päästä irti!! Let me go!!"

Suddenly I fall on my knees. My hands sink into the snow. For a brief moment I feel disoriented. Why am I on the ground?

I get up and squint as the snow hits my eyes. I hear a muted thud, then another, then another.

I turn around.

I see Greg on the ground.

Miguel is standing over him.

"If you *ever* come near her again, you're dead!! Did you hear me? *Dead!!*"

Miguel lets go of Greg's jacket and steps to the side. He takes a deep breath and sweeps the area with his eyes. Our eyes lock. He walks to me and puts his hands on my shoulders, still trying to steady his breathing.

"Are you okay?"

"Yeah, I'm fine," I say with a shaky voice.

Miguel pulls me to himself and wraps his arms around my shoulders. I look at Greg. I see him rolling to his side; blood is dripping from his face. He gets on his knees slowly. He pushes himself up. He takes a few unsteady steps and falls back on his knees. He covers his nose with his hand. Blood begins to pour through his fingers.

"You broke my nose!" he says with a voice that is both shocked and angry.

Miguel turns his head and gives Greg a look that says he should be glad he didn't break anything else.

"Fuck! I'm calling the police!"

Miguel pulls away from me and turns to look at Greg.

"Go ahead! They will charge you with attempted kidnapping and you'll go to prison for a *long* time."

"And we have proof of it."

I look in the direction of the voice. I see Jimena walking toward Greg. She's holding her phone in her hand. Greg closes his eyes briefly and pushes himself up to his feet. Jimena puts her phone in her pocket and gives Greg a look that tells him he's not worth the ground he's standing on.

"If I ever see you near Marja again, I will take the video to the police."

Greg stands in the middle of the whirling snow looking uncertain for a moment. He glances at Jimena, then at me. He wipes his nose on his jacket sleeve and makes his way to his car on unsteady legs. After a couple of tries he gets his car moving.

Jimena walks over to us. Miguel embraces her. I can hear him whisper, "*Gracias,* Jimena."

I look at Miguel. I notice he's only wearing a T-shirt.

"*Oi, rakas*.... Aren't you cold?"

Miguel turns to look at me. His eyes narrow for a second.

"What did you call me?"

I give him with a confused look.

"*Rakas*, you know, like, darling?"

"Oh, I see," he says laughing. The hardness in his eyes gives way to a smile. He puts his arm around my shoulders.

"Come on, let's go home."

I see Jimena coming from the kitchen with two beers. She hands me one. I glance toward the bedroom.

"Do you think he'll be okay?"

"Yeah, he'll be fine. He just needs to sleep a little."

I stare at the bottle for a moment.

"How did you know Greg was going to be there?" I ask carefully.

"I saw him outside the restaurant and I knew he was going to follow us. I called Miguel from the bus after you left and I asked the driver to let me out when I knew you couldn't see me. I knew it was risky, but we needed something that would stop him from coming after you and now we have it."

She pauses.

"And I needed to let Miguel do what he needed to do."

I give Jimena a look that asks what she means.

"Miguel told me about your meeting outside the courthouse. I could tell he regretted he didn't let Uncle Tino and Pablo teach your *pendejo* ex a lesson. So I figured he needed to do it himself."

Jimena's phone rings.

"*Hola, amor ... Si, ya voy.*"

Jimena gets up.

"I got to go. Carlos is here."

I get up and walk with Jimena to the front door.

"I'll see you tomorrow, ok?" says Jimena, giving me an encouraging smile.

"Yeah, I'll see you tomorrow," I say, trying to force a smile.

Jimena gives me a look.

"He won't be coming back anymore. You know that, right? You're safe now."

I nod and say good night. I close the door and walk back to the living room. I have the same feeling I had that night when Greg tried to break into my apartment, but it's not as acute. It's more like a distant flicker that becomes dimmer by the minute.

I sit down on the couch. My cat looks at me as if asking why Miguel isn't with me. It seems to have a special affinity toward him, probably because he fed it steak on the day we moved in; I forgot to bring cat food. I hug my cat for a moment. I wonder again why I accepted being treated so poorly for so long. I would never have accepted it from any man in Finland. I never let any man walk all over me at home. But of course back at home I wasn't dependent on the goodwill of a man who seemed to hate me half of the time, who thought extortion was good family values.

I pet my cat and think about going back to the church. I want to tell them exactly what Greg was like. I can already see them wriggle and blush and try to get away from the conversation with a semblance of dignity. I know men have wet dreams. Well, that's mine. But I know there would be no point to it, not really. They wouldn't listen. Not that it matters. Seeing Greg bleeding on the snowy sidewalk was enough for me. It was as if I was finally proven right. That the things he did to me were wrong, that he had no right to treat me that way.

I wish he had bled on the sidewalk a year ago.

I wouldn't have brought a tissue.

37

I wake up and glance at Miguel; he's sound asleep.

I look at my phone.

It's just past four, but I can't sleep.

I get up and go to the kitchen. I lean against the counter while I wait for the coffee to drip through the filter. I feel as if the weight of the whole world is still on my shoulders. It doesn't seem to matter what I do, I always end up afraid of something or someone. I feel endlessly tired and not just because I can't remember the last time I slept a whole night. I'm tired of the constant anxiety, the feeling I have no control over my own life.

I hope Greg has the sense to stay away. Not just because I want to stay safe, but because I don't want Miguel to get hurt ever again. I know Jimena is right. As long as she has that video, Greg won't come near me. Not because he doesn't think I deserve to be punished, but because he doesn't want to be punished himself. I can finally see him for what he is: a coward, who wanted me to be the mouse so he could be the cat. But I'm worried what Miguel will do if Greg ever does show up again. I know Miguel hates violence and that he showed restraint this time.

But I know he won't do so the next time around.

. . . . . ● . . . . .

The moment Miguel opened the door to his apartment Jimena sent him to take a hot shower and ordered him to bed right afterward. Miguel tried to argue, but she gave him one of her motherly looks.

"You were just in a fight! Look at your knuckles! How do you think you're going to feel tomorrow if you don't go to bed now?"

He shook his head, but didn't argue any further. I followed him to the bedroom. For a moment I just stood there. I didn't know what to say. I looked at his bruised right hand and felt a twinge of guilt. Miguel saw the look in my eyes. He put his arms around my shoulders and pulled me close.

"I'd do it again," he whispered. "I won't let anything bad happen to you."

I buried my head in his chest and tried to swallow the tears I knew were just waiting to fill my eyes. I couldn't help but feel I was the cause of all of this misery. If I didn't exist, none of this would ever have happened.

As if he had read my mind, Miguel grabbed my chin with his left hand. He waited until I looked him in the eyes.

"Hey, you didn't do this. *He* did. And if he ever comes near you again, he's a dead man, okay?"

I could see hardness in his eyes again.

I swallowed and nodded.

· · · · · • · · · ·

I go to the living room. I sit down on the couch and sip my

coffee slowly.

I look at my phone on the table. I wonder if there is something I could say to Greg that will finally convince him I'm not worth it. I know Miguel doesn't see it that way, but that's the whole problem. I know he'll lose it the next time and he'll end up in prison or worse. I don't want to lose Miguel, not because of Greg; not because of anything.

My phone beeps.

I pick it up and read the text.

I stare at my phone for a moment. The laughter bubbles up spontaneously as if someone has uncorked a champagne bottle. Greg tells me to stay the fuck away from him, that if I ever come near him he will have me arrested for stalking. I shake my head and type "no problems." I hit send and smile at my cat that looks at me wondering why I'm suddenly so happy.

"He's gone, for real this time. It's wonderful, isn't it? *Niin, niin ihanaa!*"

I know cats can't smile, but I'm pretty sure I can see a smile on my cat's face right now.

"Hey, why are you up?"

I turn and see Miguel by the doorway. His eyes are filled with anxiety.

"You weren't in bed and I was worried."

"You don't have to worry anymore," I say and give him my phone. "He's not coming back ever again."

Miguel sits down next to me on the couch and stares at the text for a long time. His eyes fill with tears.

"I just wouldn't be able to live with myself if something

happened to you," says Miguel wiping his eyes.

"I know. But it's okay, it's over now," I say softly.

Miguel looks at me for a long time.

"I love you more than you'll ever know."

"And I love you," I say and caress his cheek. "Would you like some breakfast?"

"It's four in the morning," says Miguel, frowning.

"So?"

"Yeah, I guess you're right, I don't think I can sleep anymore. But I have a much better idea," he says, the smile returning to his eyes.

I giggle as he leans me down on the couch.

38

I open the door to the court room.

I look around. It appears I have crashed a hearing. I stand by the door uncertain what to do. A lawyer who sits by a despondent man motions for me to go talk to the clerk. I smile briefly and walk to the woman who is shifting through papers. I give her the piece of paper and glance around the room while I wait.

I watch as a middle-aged woman gets up in the witness stand. She speaks Russian; an interpreter stands in front of the judge's bench. Her attorney begins to ask questions. The room is filled with heavy tension. I'm glad Greg and I have nothing to argue about. Our divorce will be quick compared to this one.

The clerk looks at the paper.

"Take this to room 3003. Tell them the judge here has already begun a case."

"Where is that?"

"On the 30th floor. Take the elevator."

I get out of the elevator and look around until I find the right number next to a door. I enter the room and walk to the clerk. She tells me to take a seat. I look at all the signs on the walls and on the benches. "There will be no chewing of gum in this courtroom!" says one sign. "No talking!" says the other. I can understand the need for silence, but I don't understand why they can't create waiting rooms where people can eat and drink, chew gum, and talk on their phones to keep their nerves calm and their thoughts intact. I feel jittery and I'm not even here because I'm in trouble.

The judge calls me to the bench.

"Well, Ms. Männynkoski, your application for a fee waiver is denied."

"Why?" I ask with a shocked voice.

"Because you have money in your account. Why should the good taxpayers of Cook County pay for your divorce?"

I watch as the judge writes something on the piece of paper in front of him with brisk efficiency.

"Just another reason to hate him," I say quietly.

"What did you say?"

"Nothing, it was just a joke."

"Tell me, so I can laugh too."

"Just another reason to hate him," I say loudly enough so the judge can hear me. Everyone in the room begins to laugh, except the judge.

"Well you married him, so he's all yours now."

I stare at the judge. Does he really think Greg is mine? He's not mine; he never was. I look at my shoes to hide the contempt I know has risen into my eyes. I want to ask the judge if he has forgotten I'm a taxpayer too, but I guess I haven't paid enough taxes to be considered important.

~~~~~

I leave the building and meet Jimena at the café next to the court house.

"How did it go?"

"I had to pay."

"Why? You have almost no money!"

"They thought I had enough."

"Why did you tell them how much you have?"

"They asked."

"¡*Ay,* Marja! Everybody lies! No one ever checks!"

I look at Jimena and I wish I could explain why I couldn't lie. Maybe I should have, but it just didn't feel right. I've saved most of my paycheck since I moved in with Miguel. He even insisted on giving me money for the filing fee this morning. I tried to say no, but he just shook his head. He said he didn't want me to be married to Greg a minute longer than I had to, that it was a cheap price to pay for my freedom. The look in his eyes convinced me finally.

"So, it's your birthday today! What do you two have planned for tonight?"

"Miguel said he was going to take me out to dinner."

"Oh, that's nice! But we really should go and party afterwards, don't you think?"

"Um... I think we're just going to go home."

"¿*Por que?*" asks Jimena with a frown. A split second later she smiles. "Of course you are."

I know what she's thinking and I have no reason to say she's wrong. The only difference this time is that I don't even blush as I give her the same mischievous smile I've seen on her lips more than once.

Miguel turns to his side and leans his weight against his right elbow.

"You're incredible, did you know that?" he says and slides his fingers through mine.

I just smile.

"I'm sorry we didn't get to go on our trip."

"It's okay, we can go later. Getting divorced is kind of important at this moment."

"You're right, it is. Have you decided where you would like to go later?"

"I think it would be fun to see California."

"Yeah? You want to see Hollywood?"

"I didn't say that! Isn't there more to California than Hollywood?"

"There is. I just thought that's what all tourists want to see."

"I'm not a tourist!" I say sounding more annoyed than I had intended.

"You will be and so will I."

I glance at Miguel. It's strange to think of him as a tourist in his own country, but I know he's right. California is like another country compared to Illinois, although technically it's part of the same union. It's almost like the European Union, except everyone speaks the same language here.

It makes traveling easier.

"So, when do you want to go? I'll get us tickets."

"I have to go back to court next week and I don't know how it's going to go. I mean it should be pretty straightforward, but the judge I saw today wasn't funny, so I don't know."

"Right... well, how about the beginning of May? We could go for a few days. I have vacation days I need to use up. My boss has been telling me for months to use them."

"I'll have to ask at work, but if they're okay with it, then sure."

"Great, then it's settled," smiles Miguel and releases my hand. He pulls the blanket up until it covers both of us and lies down. I turn to my side and look at him for a moment.

"Why do you like me so much?"

"What kind of question is that?" laughs Miguel, turning to look at me.

"No, I mean it. Why are you so nice to me?"

"Isn't that what I'm supposed to be?"

"I guess... it's just that—"

"You're right, not everyone is."

I glance at Miguel. I thought I hated Greg more than anyone in this world, but I'm getting the feeling Miguel's hatred tops even mine. He told me only a weak man attacks a woman. The look in his eyes told me exactly what he thought about such men. Miguel turns to his side and leans his head against his right hand.

"Why do I like you? Well, I like everything about you. You're genuine and kind. You don't pretend to be someone you're not. And there's just something about you... how to explain it... there's never any drama with you, you're just so calm all the time and it's like you can do anything you set your mind to."

"Oh, you're talking about *sisu*."

"Si—what?"

"*Sisu*. There is no way to actually translate the word, but it means if you can't go under, over, or around a rock, you go through it."

"Wow, okay, and all Finns have this thing?"

"Yes, it's hammered into us when we're children. When you live in a country that is cold and dark half of the year, you have to have it or you won't make it. You have to have ice in your veins."

"Oh, so you're an ice queen?" laughs Miguel.

"No, I'm not!" I exclaim and look away. I know I'm acting like a child, but it's what Greg used to call me when I didn't smile every time I saw him.

"Of course you're not, I was only kidding. And I think it's great you have this *sisu*, it's what I appreciate about you the most. I got tired of the drama and endless games. I guess that's why I never found anyone I could imagine spending my whole life with... until now."

I turn to look at Miguel. His eyes reflect the same surrendering love I saw in them the first time he said he loved me. I feel I'm drowning in his eyes all over again, but it's not the kind of drowning that leads to death; it's the kind of drowning that leads to merging. It's as if our souls want to become one each time we look each other in the eyes. I don't see only my own reflection in his eyes when I look at him. I see him as he truly is.

"I can't imagine spending my whole life with anyone other than you," I whisper.

"You're my whole world," says Miguel and caresses my hair. I want to tell him he's my whole world too, but he has already rolled on top of me and there's no more time for talking.

39

I enter the court house.

I feel nervous and I don't even know why. I've waited for this day for six long months. Now that it's here I feel almost like a fugitive, as if I'm still running away from my old life with Greg. I hope being officially free from him will give me the sense of freedom I haven't had for months.

"Do you have everything you need?" asks Jimena.

"I think so."

"When do you see the judge?"

"In twenty minutes."

"Good. Miguel should be here in ten minutes. I'll stay here till he comes, okay?"

I nod. I'm glad Jimena is here. I haven't seen Greg since the day he tried to kidnap me, but just knowing I'm going to have to be in the same room with him makes me nauseous. I see Greg enter the building. He glances at me but keeps on walking toward the security checkpoint. Jimena follows him with her eyes; her eyes are cold and filled with contempt. I wouldn't want to end up on the wrong side of Jimena's wrath. I guess Greg realized it too. I could tell he avoided looking at her meticulously.

"Hey, I'm not late, am I?"

I turn and see Miguel behind us. He's breathing heavily.

"No, you're actually early," says Jimena.

"Oh, good! I was afraid I was going to be late. The traffic

was a nightmare."

"Okay, well, since you're here, I'll get going. Let me know how it goes," says Jimena turning to look at me; she gives me an encouraging smile.

"I will," I say and return the smile.

We watch as Jimena leaves the building. Miguel turns to look at me.

"Do you want me to come with you?"

"No, it's okay. This shouldn't take long."

"Okay, I'll wait for you down here. Call me if you need me."

I see a flicker of anxiety in his eyes. I know he doesn't like the idea of me being alone with Greg in the same room.

I give him a kiss and walk toward the guards.

I step on the escalator and text Miguel to let him know I'm on my way.

. . . .

The judge was nice; much nicer than the previous one. He said he would let us get the dissolution papers right away. All we had to do was pay a fee to get the final decree instead of waiting the usual eight weeks. He told Greg he had to pay the back rent as he had signed the affidavit of support and also for the damaged door. Greg tried to tell the judge I had sent him a text saying I was going to kill myself because of the divorce and that he had tried to save me. The judge asked to see the text. Greg said he had accidentally deleted it. I showed the police report Jimena forced me to bring with me; I'm glad she did. The judge took one look at it and told me to get a restraining order if anything similar ever happened again. I'd never seen Greg so nonplussed. He just stared at the judge, unable to get a word out of his mouth.

. . . .

I'm about to leave the secure area when I hear someone running after me.

"Maria! Wait!"

I turn around.

Greg stops in front of me. His nose is taped and he has a nasty cut under his left eye. I didn't notice any of it before. And of course I didn't. I tried my hardest not to look at him.

"Where are you going?"

"Home," I say curtly.

"Why don't we have some coffee together?"

"Coffee?"

"Yeah, you know, for old time's sake."

I stare at Greg in disbelief.

"Are you kidding me?"

"What? Why do you have to be this way?"

I can feel anger rising from deep within. I don't even try to suffocate it.

"Why do *I* have to be *this* way? We just got divorced!" I

exclaim loudly enough that everyone around us can hear me.

"So? We can still be friends."

I look around as if I can't believe what I'm hearing.

"I don't want to be friends with you!"

"Oh, come on, Maria!"

"No, I mean it! I don't ever want to see you again!"

I turn around and begin to walk away.

"But I love you!" shouts Greg breathlessly.

I stop abruptly and turn around. I stare at Greg. *Now* he wants to talk about love, after all he's put me through? What is wrong with him? A second later it dawns on me. I'm his ex-wife and therefore unreachable. He wants me because he can't have me.

I walk back and stop a couple of steps away from him.

"I don't care what you think. We're not married anymore."

"And whose fault is that?"

"I don't care!"

"Oh, right! You want to be with your lover-boy now, don't you? Do you really think they are going to let you stay here with him?" says Greg, shaking his head. I can see his eyes mocking me.

"I actually do. I can get permanent residency myself. I don't need you."

His face turns dark.

"You ungrateful *bitch*! You didn't ever love me and I got the proof of it right here!" he says, waving the paper in his right hand.

I begin to laugh. I laugh so hard I can hardly breathe.

"You—" I say and stop to catch my breath.

"What's so funny?" asks Greg, looking at me through narrowed eyes.

"You think *I* didn't love you? *You* left me and *you* filed for the divorce, not me! Or has my English not improved enough for you to understand?"

I can tell he's stunned by his silence.

I turn around and walk away.

Goodbye Greg.

I hope I never have to see you again.

"You did what!?" says Jimena, screaming.

She reminds me of Sara, except Jimena screams when she's sober. There is nothing timid about her.

"*¡Ay cariño!* I'm so proud of you! I wish I could have seen his face!"

I laugh and shrug as to say it was no big deal. But I know it was a big deal. It was a *huge* deal. I feel as if I've grown taller by more than an inch; at least three centimeters.

"So, you're officially divorced now?"

"I am," I say smiling.

Jimena's eyes light up.

"We need to have a party! Miguel!"

Miguel comes from the kitchen. He gives me a kiss and sits down on the armrest. I glance at him. He has a relaxed look on his face.

252

"Party on Saturday, yes?"

Miguel shrugs to say "okay."

Jimena rolls her eyes.

"You need to help, dumbass!"

"Ah! I thought you have a husband."

I press my left hand against my mouth to suffocate the laughter. I can't help but find the way Miguel and Jimena spar with each other amusing. Jimena crosses her arms and gives him one of her famous annoyed looks.

"¡*Ay*, Miguel! The party is for Marja!" she says, stretching her arm in my direction.

Miguel presses his lips together and glances at me. I can see apology in his eyes.

"Okay, what do you need?"

"I'll text you a list."

I look at my phone. It's in the middle of the night, but I can't sleep. I know it's going to take a while before my natural sleep rhythm returns. Anxiety doesn't just leave in one day.

I get up and go to the living room. I leave my phone on the table and walk to the window. I look at the night sky. The night is peaceful. For once the wind isn't blowing. I watch as large snowflakes fall on the ground. It's if the angels are having a pillow fight and the filling is falling from the sky. I think of life, how it doesn't always turn out the way we think it will. I never thought I would be married and divorced by the time I was twenty-five. But then again, I didn't think I would ever live across the ocean either. I've come to realize life doesn't always turn out the way we think it will.

Sometimes it turns out better.

I came here with a dream of love and I found real love. I know I can have a real life with Miguel, a life filled with happiness and love. *Abuela* Rosalita was right, Miguel will always love me. And yet, I know it's not that simple. I love Miguel, but I don't know if I want to be an immigrant all my life, alone in a strange country without my actual family. It's not that different from being an orphan, defenseless and alone. And maybe Chicago will begin to feel like home eventually, but what if it doesn't? What if I can't assimilate enough to feel at home? My mom didn't want to live in Sweden although she always said she loved my dad. What if I'll want to go back to Finland later on and I can't? What if our love ends? What will I do then? I know Jimena is my friend, but what if Miguel decides he doesn't love me anymore? Will she still be my friend or will I end up alone all over again?

I know I have more questions than answers because life isn't like Chicago. It isn't a grid we can follow from east to west, north to south. There are no straight paths. Life gives us odd roads to follow and seemingly wrong turns to new places we never even knew existed. Maybe my life here would have turned out differently if I had met Miguel two and a half years ago instead of Greg, but there's no way of knowing and it has me going around in circles, unable to decide. But I know also that I wouldn't have met Miguel if I hadn't married Greg. So maybe it was a good thing. And maybe I shouldn't be so afraid of what will happen next. Maybe it's okay to be scared. We're all scared of something; the trick is to go ahead anyway. It's at least what Jimena has said more than once.

I know I have to make a decision soon. I know my heart wants to be with Miguel, but my heart wanted to be with Greg too. I have to be smarter than my heart this time. But what if my heart *is* right this time and this is where I'm supposed to be? Life as an immigrant is hard, but life without love is harder. Jimena was right about that one: there is no life without love. And she was right about another thing too. I did find love again.

I found Miguel.

I know I can be myself with Miguel and that he loves me more than anything. Isn't he worth it? Worth whatever it takes to make Chicago my permanent home despite of all the challenges?

"He is, in every way," I tell the night sky.

I smile to myself. It feels good to have made a decision.

I'm about to return to the bedroom when my phone beeps. I turn around and look at my phone on the table. It must be Sara. She said she was going to text me today.

I pick up my phone.

I read the texts that flood my phone.

My phone slips off my hands. It lands on the floor with a muted thud.

I gasp for air as if someone has just pushed a knife into

my back.
He found it.
He found a way to punish me.
I will never see Miguel again.

40

I watch as Jimena peels an onion.

She insisted I had to stay for lunch when I brought the groceries Miguel bought for the party. He asked me in the morning if I could bring them to Jimena before she had one of her famous hissy fits. He had to cover a shift and he didn't know when he would be back. I said I was happy to.

Jimena is about to cut the onion in half when she suddenly gives me a sharp look.

"Did you two argue? You look like you're on your way to a funeral."

"No, I—"

I close my eyes briefly and take a deep breath. I know I have to tell her the truth.

"I'm going back to Finland. I bought the ticket this morning."

Jimena puts the knife down.

"You're going back? Why?"

"Because I have to."

"But what about Miguel? I've never seen him like this! He is *completely* in love with you! I'm sure he's going to buy you a ring soon! Don't you love him?"

"I do, but…"

"Then why are you leaving?"

"I—"

"*Listen!* Long distance relationships are hard, *too* hard. I know all about it! Don't do this to yourself! You have to stay!"

"I can't!"

"Why not!"

I look away for a moment.

"Remember that day when you told me I had to end it with Greg and I told you if I did they would send me home?"

Jimena presses her lips together and looks away. I can tell she has forgotten all about it.

"We're divorced now so I have to go home."

Jimena puts her fingertips over her mouth and shakes her head.

"This isn't right. Are you sure there isn't *any* way you can stay? I mean, there has to be!"

"There is, but—"

The light returns to Jimena's eyes. She wipes her hands on a towel and sits down next to me.

"I knew it! Let's hear it!"

I feel my throat constrict.

"I—I can apply for permanent residency on my own, but I have to prove that Greg left me and that he went back to his ex-wife."

"Well that's simple, he did!"

"I know, but how do I prove it?

"I can send Uncle Tino to get the evidence, no problems," says Jimena waving her hand in the air as if it was the easiest thing in the world.

"Okay... Then I have to show that I would, uh, have economic hardship if I'm sent back home."

"Well, can you?"

"Not really."

"That's okay. We'll just make something up."

"And then there's the application. It costs money, a lot of money."

"Forget about the money! Do you think Miguel is going to let you leave over a few dollars?"

"It's not just a few dollars. It's hundreds of dollars."

"Who cares? He'll pay whatever is needed. Is that it?"

"No, um—"

I look at my hands.

"Greg isn't going to let me stay," I say quietly.

"And why does that worm think he has any say in it?" asks Jimena with biting contempt in her voice.

"He... um... texted me yesterday and said if I don't go home, he is going to accuse me of adultery and they will deny my application because of it."

"Adultery?"

"He said he's going to tell the immigration officials that I had an affair with Miguel and that it destroyed our marriage and that's why he divorced me."

Jimena looks at me as if she hasn't understood a word I've said.

"But *he* was the one who left *you*."

"I know, but he's going to say he came back and wanted to make it work, but that I didn't want to because of Miguel."

"Okay, but you met Miguel *after* he came back, we all know this!"

"He's going to say I met him while we were separated."

"Oh my God, that's total bullshit! How does he think he's going to prove any of it?"

"He knows I was on Tinder. He's going to say I met Miguel there."

"How does he know you were on Tinder?" asks Jimena, looking at me through narrowed eyes. "Ah, never mind. He was there himself, wasn't he?"

"I think so, but I can't prove it."

"Okay, but how can *he* prove that *you* were there?"

"He took screenshots. He sent them to me last night."

"Screenshots? I can't believe this! That bastard abandoned you, tried to kidnap you, and *he* gets to accuse *you*?!" exclaims Jimena, looking to the right the way she always does when she's seething. She shakes her head and mutters something in Spanish. I can only hear the word *madre*; the rest escapes me. Suddenly she turns to look at me. She looks startled as if something has taken her by surprise.

"Does he have any other evidence?"

"I don't know. He didn't mention anything else."

"So, if I hadn't created that Tinder account for you, he wouldn't have anything on you? You'd be able to stay?"

"Maybe, I don't know."

Jimena looks away and stares into nothingness for a long time. When she turns to look at me again, her eyes are drained of all life.

"Have you told Miguel yet?"

"No, I'm going to tell him tonight."

Jimena gets up and walks over to me. She gives me a hug and leaves the kitchen without a word.

I return from the bathroom and sit down on the couch. I stare at my hands for a moment.

"I—I have to tell you something."

"What is it?" asks Miguel, turning to look at me. His eyes are so full of love that I have to look away for a moment. I force myself to look at him again.

"I'm… I'm going to Finland."

"Oh? For how long?"

I close my eyes briefly.

"I'm not coming back."

Miguel looks as if someone has just taken a baseball bat to his stomach.

"What do you mean?"

"I had only a conditional residency. I lost it because I got divorced before I was married for two years."

Miguel looks confused for a moment. Slowly the light returns. He leans his head back and closes his eyes briefly.

"*That's* why he divorced you as soon as he could…"

He shakes his head and says something in Spanish. I don't know what the words mean, but I've heard Jimena say them a few times when she's been mad. I assume he's cursing.

"Why didn't you tell me before?" he asks, turning to look at me. I can see both shock and disbelief in his eyes.

"I—I thought I would be able to stay, but I found out yesterday that I can't."

"When do you leave?"

"In two days."

"Two—"

Miguel takes a few shallow breaths as if he's just lost the ability to breathe. He gets up and paces the floor a few times, sits back down on the couch and covers his nose and mouth with his hands. He looks as if all air has just left him.

"I'm sorry," I say with a voice barely louder than a whisper.

Miguel sweeps the room with his eyes as if he's looking for someone to tell him this is just some great cosmic joke. He turns to look at me, trying to still steady his breathing.

"And you're absolutely sure you can't stay?"

"I have to file for the removal of conditions ninety days before my conditional residency expires and I need to be married to do it."

"That's no problem!" exclaims Miguel. "I'll marry you! We can go to City Hall tomorrow!"

"I need to be married to Greg."

I can see the glimmer of hope vanish from his eyes. He slides his hands through his hair.

"But why do you have to leave so soon? Can't you stay a little longer?"

"I have till September, but I quit my job this morning."

"I'll take care of you!"

"We would just be counting the days. I don't think I can do that," I say quietly.

"Then why don't I come to Finland with you?" says Miguel, spreading his arms as if he's just found the obvious solution.

"I don't think you'd like it."

"Why not?"

"You would have to learn Finnish and it's hard for foreigners to find work."

"Okay, how about Mexico? We could move there!"

"How? How would we get visas there?"

"I don't know. It was just an idea."

Miguel presses the top of his nose with his left thumb and index finger. He shakes his head as if he can't believe any of it.

"I just wish I could prove Greg left me first. If I could prove it, then they might let me stay."

Miguel turns to look at me. His eyes are wide as if he's trying to take in what I just said.

"What do you mean?"

"Sara told me I can apply for permanent residency by myself with a waiver—"

"Well, why don't you!"

I look at Miguel. He looks like a child on Christmas morning, waiting to open presents. I look away for a moment. I know what I'm about to say is going to make him feel there isn't going to be another Christmas ever again.

"I can apply, but there are no guarantees they will

approve it. I have to prove Greg abandoned me and went back to his ex-wife. They're going to talk to him and I know he's going to make it look like I used him to get a Green Card."

I pause for a moment.

"And they're going to believe him, because he's going to accuse me of adultery because of you."

"Me?"

Miguel looks at me as if he's not sure he heard me right. Slowly the surprise gives way to the realization he's the reason I can't stay.

"You mean, if we had waited—"

"If we had waited I would have no reason to stay. I'd be going home anyways."

Miguel covers his face with his hands for a moment. When he turns to look at me his eyes are filled with indescribable pain.

"I just don't know how I'm going to live without you."

"I don't know how I'm going to live without you either," I say, trying to stop the tears.

My cat jumps on the couch and tries to get on my lap.

My cat!

I had forgotten all about it. I let my cat form itself into a ball on my lap. I pet it for a moment.

"Do you know anyone who would like my cat?"

"I'll keep it," says Miguel and tries to smile.

"Are you sure?"

"It'll remind me of you."

Tears flood my eyes, I can't stop them anymore. I

continue to pet my cat as tears stream down my face. I wish I could go back to January and tell Miguel the truth. If I had been honest maybe our love story would have ended differently.

But even I know it's not true.

There never was another ending to our love story than this.

41

Carlos opens the door.

"Miguel! Marja! *¡Bienvenidos!* Come in, come in!"

We enter the small hallway. Carlos takes a couple steps toward the bedroom.

"¡Jimena, están aquí!"

"¡Un momentito! ¡Necesito encontrar mis aretes!"

Carlos shakes his head and gives us an apologetic smile.

"Jimena will come soon. She has lost her earrings. I think I must buy her a bigger box for her jewelry."

I laugh and take off my jacket. Miguel hangs it up for me and walks with me to the living room.

"Would you like something to drink?"

"Yeah, sure."

Miguel goes to the corner and brings me a beer. Jimena comes to the living room. She's wearing a sleek black dress and her long hair rests on her left shoulder. She gives both of us a kiss on the cheek.

"*Abuela* Rosalita has been cooking all day. She insisted when I told her the party was for Marja."

"Then it's good. I'll be right back," says Miguel and goes to the kitchen.

I glance at Jimena. She seems subdued.

"Is something wrong?" I ask carefully.

"Of course something's wrong! You're leaving!"

exclaims Jimena as tears begin to stream down her face.

She wipes her eyes carefully to avoid messing up her makeup.

"And I know it's my fault," she whispers, glancing toward the kitchen to see if Miguel is within earshot.

"No, it isn't!"

"Yes, it is! If I hadn't created that Tinder account for you, you and Miguel could be together! He will never forgive me when he finds out and he's *never* going to talk to me again! Oh, God… this is so awful."

"Jimena, don't blame yourself, *please!* He would have found something else! He knows how to lie."

Jimena looks at me and shakes her head.

"It's still my fault. I just can't believe that *bastard* is getting away with this! They should send *him* away instead!"

"Yeah, well, it's not how this works."

"I know, but I'm going to miss you so much!"

Jimena gives me a hug. She holds me tight, a little too tight. My eyes mist. I don't even want to know what my life would have been the past few months without Jimena.

"I'm going to miss you too," I whisper, trying to hold back the tears.

Jimena pulls away and fans her face with her right hand.

"But hey! You'll get to go back to the happiest country in the world!"

I laugh.

"I don't think Finns see it that way."

"What do you mean?" asks Jimena with a confused look.

"I mean, I think we are content rather than happy."

Jimena shakes her head and rolls her eyes.

"¡*Ay,* Marja! *¡Es lo mismo!* It's the same!"

I laugh. I can tell she is beginning to feel more like herself.

"Maybe you're right."

"Of course I'm right! I'm always right!" says Jimena, her smile returning.

I laugh again. The laughter is followed by a sharp pain somewhere near my heart. I know I'll never see Jimena again. We'll both swear we'll visit each other and we'll send Christmas cards, e-mails, and texts for a few years, but with time our friendship will fade into oblivion.

"Is Miguel taking you to the airport?"

"Yeah, we're taking the train."

"I hope you don't mind if I don't come. I hate saying goodbye, especially at the airport. It's just *so* depressing."

"Of course I don't."

Jimena wipes her eyes again.

"Oh, why am I crying? It's a party! Come, let's get something to drink."

The taxi stops in front of the apartment building. Miguel helps me out of the car.

I feel nearly completely sober although I've had more than enough to drink. I breathe in the cold night air. It's the last time I'll do so here in Chicago. It feels odd. I've wanted to go home for so long, and now that I'm about to leave, all I can think is how much I want to stay.

We enter Miguel's apartment. I take off my shoes and put my jacket in the closet.

I see Miguel standing in the middle of the living room. I walk over to him and put my hand on his arm.

"Hey…"

Miguel turns around and kisses me like there is no tomorrow. He walks me to the bedroom, still kissing me. He begins to pull my dress off with impatient hands. I pull his shirt up halfway; he pulls it over his head and throws it on the floor. He wraps his arms around my waist and kisses me again. He kisses my neck and buries his head against my shoulder. I can hear his heavy breathing.

I caress his back and whisper "I love you."

"*Te amo, te amo…*" he says in a muffled voice as if he can't say it enough times.

I glance at my phone. It's seven in the morning.

I move Miguel's arm gently to the side and get up. I go to the living room and sit down by the dining room table.

I stare at the paper.

It's my ticket home.

By this time tomorrow I'll be back in Finland. I'll return to my old life and it will be as if none of this ever happened, as if I had never met Greg, Jimena, or Miguel. They will all be just part of a dream that never was, my beautiful dream that I thought for a moment had become reality. Their memory will fade with time and they will become part of a story I will tell to my grandchildren, if I ever have children of my own.

"What are you doing up?"

I turn my head and see Miguel by the bedroom door.

"I couldn't sleep," I say, trying to smile.

Miguel rubs his neck with his left hand and walks slowly to the table. He sits down and stares at the piece of paper. His eyes are filled with something inexpressible.

"So that's it? I'll never see you again."

"Don't say that."

"But it's true."

I brush his hair away from his forehead and give him a weak smile.

"What did you tell me? That it's better to have lost love than never have loved?"

"I don't believe that anymore," says Miguel quietly, getting up. He walks to the window and stares at the view for a long time. When he turns to look at me, his eyes are filled with despair.

"Don't go, *please*...."

"They'll deport me if I don't leave," I say with a voice that is firmer than I intended.

"I—"

Miguel rubs his neck again and stares at the floor for a moment.

"I just don't understand why you can't stay."

"It's how it works."

"So he's allowed to abuse you and there's nothing anyone can't do about it?"

I look at my hands.

"It's not supposed to happen," I say quietly.

"But it did! So why don't we do something about it?"

"He'll just lie and tell them it was my fault, all of it!"

"We can challenge him!"

"You don't know Greg like I do. He'll do *anything* to send me back home!"

"But we can fight it! We can get a lawyer! I'll borrow the money if I have to!"

"And what if we lose? I know he wants to punish me for leaving him and for loving you. You would have spent all that money and I would have to go back home anyways!"

"I don't care!"

"But I do! It would mean Greg gets to punish you too! I won't let him!"

"He already is," whispers Miguel and turns to look out the window again.

I cover my face with my hands and close my eyes. I can feel a tear fall on my palms, then another. I wish I was brave, but I'm not. I can't imagine spending months trying to defend myself against Greg's lies knowing he'll win and that my heart will be broken all over again. I'd rather go home now than later. It will hurt less that way.

I can feel Miguel's hand on my shoulder.

"Let's go back to bed," he says with a quiet voice.

42

The train makes a screeching sound as it approaches the end station. We get off the train and get on the escalator. Miguel is quiet. I wish he would say something, but I know there's nothing he could say.

We make our way through the maze that is O'Hare and enter the international departure hall.

Miguel taps my shoulder.

"Hey, I need to use the restroom. I'll be right back."

I watch as Miguel walks across the hall.

I look at the piece of paper in my hand.

I turn to look at the travelers who walk up and down the large departure hall.

I look at the airline people smiling behind the counters.

I look at the people who hug and cry and say goodbye.

The thought comes to me as if it has traveled a long distance and has finally caught up with me.

I've been saying goodbye all my life. To my dad when I was little, to every boyfriend I've ever had, my best friend, every person I've ever loved. I didn't choose every goodbye, but I've been running ever since the first one. I've been running from love, running from it before it can hurt me again. But the more I've been running, the more I've been hurt.

I can't keep on running anymore.

I look at the people who are all on their way somewhere.

Some people are going home.

But I *am* home.

Miguel is my home.

I've never been brave, but I don't need to be brave to stay home. Crossing the ocean takes bravery, being at home doesn't. It requires staying power; it requires *sisu*, something every Finn has. And I don't want everyone else around me to continue to win. I especially don't want Greg to win anymore.

I want to win this time.

"Hey, we should get you into the line, it's becoming long."

I look at Miguel who has returned and seems to want get the whole thing over and done with.

"You said something about wanting to fight it."

Miguel looks as if lightning has struck the building. His eyes betray both surprise and despair.

"I want to stay, here, with you."

Miguel looks at me. Tears begin to fall down his cheeks. He grabs me and hugs me so tight I can barely breathe.

"You mean it?" he asks between the sobs.

"I do. I love you," I say just before tears make speaking impossible.

"I love you," whispers Miguel. He pulls away until he can see my eyes. He looks at me through the tears.

"We'll win, okay?"

He cups my face with his hands and kisses me like there is a tomorrow.

Acknowledgments

I wish to extend a heartfelt thank you to Finlandia Foundation National for believing in me and this project, and for your kind contribution.
Kiitos

I wish to say an endless thank you to my mom and dad, who've supported me in more ways than I can count, who are my greatest cheerleaders, and who I have always been able to count on, even from the other side of the world.
Kiitos

I wish to also extend a special thanks to my friend Mirta Jackson, who found me just in time and who walked me through the muddy waters of finding myself all over again when I was lost in the swamp of uncertainty.
Kiitos

I wish to thank all of my teachers in Finland for teaching me the English language the hard way. I wouldn't be a writer today if it wasn't for all the incredible, unassuming, brilliant teachers who loved the language and had enough *sisu* to teach me all the rules, whether I wanted it or not. I didn't understand the value of your commitment until now.
Kiitos

And I wish to thank all the Finnish women in the USA I've met in the virtual world who taught me all over again that being a Finn is a beautiful thing. You are too numerous to mention by name, but I will never forget your kindness and love, and our wonderful discussions.

Kiitos

And finally, this book is written with gratitude to every immigrant who has ever braved the prejudice and discrimination that comes with moving to a new country. It's one of the hardest decisions a person can make, but it can also be one the best decisions a person can make. The difference lies in how we see ourselves. So, to all of you brave immigrants who dared to dream and paved the way for the rest of us with your endless resilience—

Kiitos,
Thank You

SANAKIRJA
Glossary of Finnish & Spanish
words and phrases found in this novel
(Numbers refer to chapters)

1

Voi vittu – Oh, fuck!

2

Sä oot kuin meiän mummo! Nyt pistät hameen päälle ja tuut tänne – You're like my grandma! Get dressed and get over here!

Ok, mä tuun – Okay, I'm coming.

Katriina, perkele! Sunhan piti auttaa mua ennen tenttiä! Minne helvettiin sä katosit? – Katriina, what the hell? You promised to help me before the exam! Where the hell did you go?

Eikö se riitä jo? – Isn't enough already?

4

Älä liiku! – Don't move!

5

¡Hola, cariño! – Hi, sweetie!

Extraña – Strange, weird

Por supuesto – Of course

7

Vitun idiootti – Fucking idiot!

Vitun viini! – Fucking wine!

8

Voi saatana! Miksi mä luotin suhun? – Damn! Why did I trust you?

10

¡Lo siento, cariño! - I'm sorry, sweetie!

Perfecto! – Perfect!

18

Abuela – Grandma

Menudo – Traditional Mexican soup

19

Dios Mio – Oh, my God

22

Estupido – Stupid

24

Eres la mujer más hermosa del mundo… te amo – You are the most beautiful woman in the whole world… I love you.

Mä rakastan sua – I love you

25

Andiamo! – Here we go!

Prego! – You're welcome!

Saraa hyvää tulee — Lit. slowly good things are created

28

Hola, mi amor – Hello, my love

32

Mi amiga – My friend

Mucho gusto – Nice to meet you

36

Hola, amor… Si, ya voy – Hello, love… yes, I'm coming

41

¡Jimena, están aquí! – Jimena, they are here!

¡Un momentito! Necesito encontrar mis aretes! – One moment! I need to find my earrings!